Life of a Savage 4

Romell Tukes

Lock Down Publications and Ca$h
Presents

Life of a Savage 4

A Novel by *Romell Tukes*

Romell Tukes

Lock Down Publications
P.O. Box 944
Stockbridge, Ga 30281
www.lockdownpublications.com

Copyright 2022 Romell Tukes
Life of a Savage 4

First Edition September 2022
Printed in the United States of America

Lock Down Publications
Like our page on Facebook: Lock Down Publications @
www.facebook.com/lockdownpublications.ldp
Book interior design by: **Shawn Walker**
Edited by: **Mia Rucker**

Stay Connected with Us!

Text **LOCKDOWN** to 22828 to stay up-to-date with new releases, sneak peaks, contests and more…
Thank you!

Romell Tukes

Submission Guideline.

Submit the first three chapters of your completed manuscript to ldpsubmissions@gmail.com, subject line: Your book's title. The manuscript must be in a .doc file and sent as an attachment. Document should be in Times New Roman, double spaced and in size 12 font. Also, provide your synopsis and full contact information. If sending multiple submissions, they must each be in a separate email.

Have a story but no way to send it electronically? You can still submit to LDP/Ca$h Presents. Send in the first three chapters, written or typed, of your completed manuscript to:

LDP: Submissions Dept
P.O. Box 944
Stockbridge, Ga 30281

DO NOT send original manuscript. Must be a duplicate.

Provide your synopsis and a cover letter containing your full contact information.

Thanks for considering LDP and Ca$h Presents.

Acknowledgements

First and foremost, all praises are due to the most high, Allah. Big thanks to all my readers and supporters. Much love. I will forever be the HOV of the pen game. Facts (LOL). Shout out to Yonkers, NY, my bro CB, Lingo Loc, Baby James, Brisco, King Hound, Smurf, Frazier, and the Cartels. Shout out to my BK guys: OG Chuck, Tails, Gunny, Flatbush guys, and my East NY guys. Shout out to KD from Trenton, NJ on HSH, shout to Peterson, NJ - Beast, Rugar, Nap, T-Burn, Sha Brim and B.G. Shout out to Miami, ATL, Texas, LA; coast to coast vibes. Big shout out to LDP and Cas$h for the support and devotion they put into making stars. Free da real men and women locked down. Use your time wisely. Everybody in the free world, never take life for granted. It's short. Enjoy it with the ones you love. Sit back and enjoy this book. It's a movie, you heard. Hood classic type vibez.

Romell Tukes

Prologue
Miami, FL.
Years ago

A federal agent had just left Savage's house a couple of minutes ago, informing Britt that her brother Jo Jo's murder case was going cold. The agent informed her that they found a lot of shell casings that were emptied outside from a .357 handgun. Jo Jo was shot with a .357 which left no shells, so she knew somebody was sending a message. The agent instructed her to give him a call ASAP if she heard anything that could be useful.

Once the agent left, Britt started to cry like a baby. She knew for a fact that Savage and his crew were the only team to use .357; it was their trademark. The whole Mimia knew.

Britt grabbed a duffle bag from her closet that was already downstairs. She told the guards to look after him before leaving.

***

South Miami, FL

Savage drove to the graveyard to see his mother's tombstone and to pay her a visit. Today was the anniversary of her death so he had to come up here. Savage felt as if it was all fault that his friends and family were dead. He had a bottle of Henny with him in his passenger seat and two .357 handguns pulling up to the main entrance of the graveyard.

Walking to his mother's grave he felt like his life was at a dead-end. He took a sip out the bottle as tears rolled down his face and dark clouds started to come together forming over his head.

"Mom, I'm sorry. I'm done with this lifestyle. I'm taking care of Lil Smoke and I'ma try my best to be a good husband. I deserve to give my family that of Allah's will." Savage poured out some Henny, talking to his mom's grave. He looked at Rich's grave next to hers. Savage thought he heard footsteps but when he reached for his guns, he realized he'd left them in his car.

"I'm glad you made it. I've been waiting today all day because today is the day I killed her sexy ass, remember?" Killer asked, pointing a gun at him, four feet behind him.

"Just to get back at me," Savage said as he took a sip out his bottle, looking Killer in his eyes.

"You destroyed my empire," Killer said.

"You should never go up against a savage. But before you kill me, I think you should know your my blood brother," says Savage with a serious face.

"That's not finna save you, fuck boy," Killer stated.

"Our father name is Tone. He was murdered Feb 10, 1990, the day I was born. Your mother is Jessica, my mother Lisa's best friend," Savage said as Killer lowered his weapon because he knew the story just as well. Tears came down Savage's face as he told the rest of the story.

As soon as they were about to embrace, Killer's head was blown off his shoulders, splashing blood all over Savage's face. He picked up Killer's pistol and aimed it at the shooter who had a gun already aimed at him with a crazy look in her eyes.

"What the fuck wrong with you? Put the gun down, Britt," Savage said as they stood there staring at each other with their guns aimed on each other.

"No," she said.

"That was my brother!"

"Good, now we almost even, bitch." She had an evil stare.

"What? I didn't kill Jo Jo. Believe me. Put the gun down, please. I love you," Savage stated.

"Oh yeah, just like you loved Jada. Yeah, I killed that bitch Randall. I saw y'all was creeping to hotels. You loved her, too," Britt said through tears.

"I'm sorry, Britt, that was a mistake. I gave my life to you," he said crying with her.

Britt wanted to pull the trigger so badly but she couldn't do it. His words sounded so sincere to her as she lowered her .357. Britt walked towards Savage but bullets from nowhere ripped through her body. Her last words were, "Love you," as she fell in front of his feet, with her .357 felling out her hand.

Once Savage saw she was gone, he saw Bama standing there. "I thought she was about to kill you," Bama said.

Savage aimed his gun at Bama while Bama aimed his gun back.

"What the fuck?" Said Bama

"You killed my wife. It's a life for a life, friends or not," Savage stated.

"You are trying to kill me over a bitch?"

Savage shot him in his shoulder, but out of left field, Khadija came busting bullets from a high-powered gun, hitting Savage over ten times in his chest.

"You saved my life, baby. How did you know I was here?" Bama asked, rubbing his wound.

"I followed you," she said, going into her backpack, pulling out a snake and tossing it on Savage's body.

Bama was confused. He planned to talk to her about the snake shit later.

"We gotta get to a hospital or Dr. Ali ASAP, baby. I'm losing a lot of blood," Bama said in pain.

"I don't think you will make it," Khadija said in a soft tone as she quickly disarmed him and roundhouse kicked him, making him fall. "Big Zoe paid me years ago to kill your crew and I always complete my mission, baby. I did love you, baby. I promise my love for you is real. I'll see you."

Tat … Tat … Tat … Tat … Tat … Tat …

She shot him six times in the chest while crying. As she turned around, she saw SWAT trucks and FBI agents all swarming the area with guns out screaming, "Freeze!"

Khadija smiled and got on one knee, acting as if she was about to surrender. Instead, she let off shots from her weapon, killing four agents on the scene.

The police fired back but she ran into the woods at a fast pace leaving no trace.

Romell Tukes

Chapter 1
Dade County, FL
Years Later

Lil Smoke parked outside of a Caribbean restaurant watching it closely in the driver seat of his old model Ford Escape. It was 9:30PM night and the restaurant closed at 10, so he waited patiently for his lick to pull up. Lil Smoke had been watching the spot for the last two months since he graduated high school. He leaned back in his seat, listening to rap music, thinking about what his life was like now since growing up under Yasir.

Since his brother died, Yasir was left to raise him and his own family. Growing up without a mom and dad, he was focused on teaching himself the street life. Yasir raised him in an Islamic household with his own son Nafee who'd just graduated college, and with Lil Smoke out of school, they had been chilling a lot.

Lil Smoke wanted to get some money now and the first thing that came to his mind was robbing. Every day he thought about Britt and Savage. When he heard the story how a female assassin killed his brother and got away, he got upset.

The man he was waiting on was named Pain— a Haitian man who sold drugs out of his restaurant.

Lil Smoke's friend he went to school with was Pain's little brother, so when he to talked about Pain all day, Lil Smoke used to listen.

Going to college was out of the question for him. Lil Smoke wanted some fast money and he planned to get it out the mud. Laying on a nigga was something he heard in rap songs or saw on movies, but this was his first steak out. He was going to call his best friend Lil Trap on this mission, but he decided against it and to go alone. Being his first mission, he wanted to get a feel of how it was going to be. He heard stories of his older brother and how he had one of the most dangerous crews in Miami.

He saw a Rolls Royce pull up to the restaurant and two men hopped out in fancy suits with dreads.

***

South Miami

Pain began a hustler at an early age; he was Haitian and Jamaican, so he had the best of both worlds. He washed his dirty money by opening a few restaurants in Miami, his hometown. Everybody thought Pain was the real plug, but he was only the middleman. His brother KVon was the real drug connect, but he was focused on his businesses he had throughout Miami.

Pain and his cousin got out of the car and walked into the restaurant to pick up something from the safe to drop off to KVon. "Close the place up," Pain told the manager when he saw one customer sitting down eating.

"Yes, sir," the Haitian women stated, doing as the owner said.

"Troppy, grab me a duffle bag from the kitchen and meet me in the office." Pain told his cousin.

"Got'cha!" Trophy shouted, walking off, chewing on a toothpick.

Once in the back, Pain opened the safe and saw big stacks of money in rows. "Money, money, money …" Pain sung until he saw his cousin walk into the room with his hands up. "What the fuck!" Pain shouted when he saw Lil Smoke with a .357 handgun to the back of Troppy's head.

His older brother Savage's trademark gun was the .357, so Lil Smoke felt it was only right to let the legacy continue. "Don't move and nobody will get hurt," Lil Smoke stated, tossing Pain the duffle bag to fill up with the money he saw in the safe.

"Listen, little bruh, you making a big mistake here," Pain said.

"Nigga, what? I look like I need a fucking pep-talk? T-Pain in the face ass nigga, bag that paper up, bruh."

Lil Smoke almost made Troppy laugh because his cousin was an ugly ass nigga.

"Aight." Pain quickly placed the money in the bag, hoping the young man wouldn't shoot.

"That's everything?" Lil Smoke looked into the now empty safe.

"Yeah."

"No, it's not. Both of you hoe ass niggas drop y'all watches in there, and them gold teeth," Lil Smoke said as they did as he asked.

"That's all we got," Troppy said before the gun blast blew his head juices all over the office wall and table.

Pain almost had a heart attack because he knew he was next, especially when he saw the lost soul in Lil Smoke's eyes.

BOOM! BOOM! BOOM! BOOM!

Lil Smoke fired four rounds in his face, killing him. He picked up the bag and left out the front door. When he came in minutes ago, he let the manager and customer leave. He didn't believe in killing or hurting women who did not deserve it.

Back inside of his car, he drove off, checking the time. He knew he would make it home for the night prayer called Isha. He planned to hide the money until he came up with a solid idea to invest it or flip it. The first person he planned to pull up on was Lil Trap in a few days.

Romell Tukes

Chapter 2
Palm Beach County, FL

Khadija woke up from a long night's sleep, something she rarely got these days because not only she was extremely busy, but it's been hard for her to sleep with all the dirt she's done.

Ramadan had just passed two days ago which was a 30 day fast for Muslims.

She stretched in her apartment bedroom, looking around at all the assault rifles and pet tanks. The pet tanks she had all over her crib were filled with black African snakes and king cobra's that could spit venom up to six feet and kill a person. Khadija loved her snakes more than her weapons.

Looking at herself in the mirror she admired how beautiful she was with her smooth honey brown skin, gray eyes which were exotic, her curves, long hair and her perky breast. She spent five days a week exercising in the gym or sometimes she would go to the nearby park.

Being full blooded African, she was strong in her black beauty and exotic features which was rare. She was getting older in her 30's but she still looked no older than twenty-one.

Her father Umer was still in Africa controlling the drug trade in the motherland. Since he had her kill Savage and her husband Bama who was Savage's best friend, her and Umer's relationship had been rocky and distant.

The day she killed her husband she also killed a few FBI agents at the scene, so she'd been laying low for over a decade. She had lots of money in her bank accounts that could last her a lifetime.

Her father's birthday was in a few weeks and she planned to go pay her brother a visit.

Khadija spent most of her days on beaches, shopping, spas, traveling, and enjoying life. Her last relationship was last year with a Muslim man who owned an Islamic bookstore, but he wanted to marry her, and she wasn't ready to re-marry. That relationship didn't last long at all; it was good for her to get her rocks off. She still had Bama's wedding ring he gave her. Every day she thought about him. If she could bring back the hands of time, she would to bring him back.

Khadija prepared for her morning exercise and made herself a breakfast shake.

***

South Miami, FL

Days later…

KVon got out his all-black Porsche taking off his sunglasses, about to attend his little brother's wake in a South Miami church. KVon was a low-key kingpin nigga who ran a few small businesses to keep a low profile from the feds and the street niggas. He looked like a model— tall, dark skin, muscular, and a handsome face. He loved his Haitian and Jamaican culture just like he loved his little brother.

Pain controlled the streets for him the right way with his crew they called Top Six.

Walking into the church he saw his aunty talking to his little cousin Do Do who a shooter. "Do Do," KVon said in his low voice.

"Cuz, I'm sorry about what happened," Do Do said sadly because he looked up to KVon and Pain growing up.

"Fuck all dat sorrow shit. Save that for my mom. This is what I need you and your crew to do for me, to bring real justice to Pain."

"Anything, bruh," Do Do said, knowing his crew was down for any type of drama.

"I want you to go review the cameras at the restaurant and find out who ran up in the spot."

"That's all, bruh?"

"Find out who did it, then bring them to me." KVon stated.

"I got you."

"You're taking over his spot. You know the rules to the game." KVon saw his mom come over and started speaking to him in Creole.

KVon spent rest of the day grieving with his family, assuring them it will be okay, and he will find the killers or killer.

Later that night he got a call from his drug connect Royal who took over Montanta Cartel. A long time ago after the big war between Goya and Montanta, he was his nephew.

Romell Tukes

Chapter 3
South Miami, FL

Nafee rode in his Impala listening to Kodak Black, thinking about his job interview he was on his way to. A few months ago, Nafee graduated from Florida State University and he earned his Business Degree. College life was the best experience he ever encountered; he only wished Lil Smoke would've been able to see how it was, but he planned to let him make that choice on his own. Nafee called Lil Smoke his little brother because he grew up with him. They shared the same room in his father Yasir's crib and they did everything together.

At 21 years old, soon to be 22, he knew what he wanted to do in life. He had his head in the right direction. He was a handsome young man— tall, brown skin, short but wavy hair, and a nice smile. He was a woman magnet. With no wife or kids, he felt like he was in a good position to do as he pleased. Nafee was a born Muslim and he practiced his religion by praying five times a day, fasting, and following the Islamic rules. His father Yasir basically had him and Lil Smoke living in the mosque. Growing up in an Islamic household was very strict and hard on him, but it kept him and Lil Smoke out of trouble.

Since being home from college he had been living with his dad, but Nafee was ready to have his own spot and live his own life. With no money, he had no choice but to live with Yasir who still treated him like a kid.

He pulled into Walmart shopping center twenty minutes before his interview with the manager. While in college he never thought he would be hoping for a job at Walmart, but he had no choice right now. Nafee wore a button up and a pair of slacks with shoes hoping to land the job.

Walking into Walmart he saw it was full of shoppers. He walked up to one of the employees. "Excuse me, do you know where I can find Mr. Sonvia?" Nafee asked the young woman who looked familiar.

"Nafee?" She asked.

"Yes, that's me."

"It's me. Donna."

"Donna? Oh shit!" Nafee couldn't believe how bad she was looking with a stomach hanging over her belt and bags under her eyes. Donna use to be one of the baddest bitches in high school. He always wanted to fuck her.

"You looking good. I heard you went to college."

"Yep."

"Okay. I had two kids with Max but he locked up now doing life in prison for killing my ex-boyfriend," she said as if she didn't care.

"Max? The best high school quarterback in Miami back then?" Nafee asked.

"Yeah."

"Damn, bruh."

"Yeah, but what's up with you? Take a bitch out on a date or somthin'," she said.

Nafee smelled her stanky breath and tried not to cover his mouth or hold his breath. "I'll get back with you on that, but where can I find the manager?"

"Oh, yeah, near the food court section." She pointed to the far right.

"Thank you." Nafee made his way to the manager's office to see a white man out front talking to a younger white kid, telling him he starts next week after his piss test comes back. "Are you Mr. Sonvia?" He asked.

"Yes, who are you?" Sonvia shot back, looking him up and down.

"Nafee, and I have an interview with you today. We spoke briefly yesterday," Nafee said.

"Oh, yes. Nafee, I'm sorry, but that position has been filled."

"What?"

"I believe that position has been filled, sir," Mr. Sonvia said.

"But you told me over the phone you had a few positions open," Nafee stated, seeing Sonvia look on the clipboard he had in his hand.

"I don't recall."

"I need a job, Mr. Sonvia. I'm fresh outta college, broke, and I'm willing to work my ass off."

"I understand, but we're just not hiring right now," Sonvia lied.

"I just saw you hire that white kid." Nafee was starting to get upset.

"Listen, we don't need no more black people... I mean *young* people working in here. I'm sorry." Sonvia tried to correct his racist remark.

"Black people," Nafee said before he punched Sonvia in his face, knocking him out clean and leaving the store. Nafee walked past Donna who saw the whole show and she was turned on.

Nafee never thought it would be hard to get a job at Walmart these days with a college degree. He felt like he didn't have the right complexion for the connection. He wondered why he even went to college if he wasn't even qualified to get a job at Walmart. Driving home he played some new Yo Gotti and Moneybagg Yo, trying to figure out his next move because he was flat broke.

***

North Shore, Miami

Nafee saw his dad's truck parked in the front yard, but he knew soon he had to go to work. His dad owned a plumbing company and made good money. Yasir wanted Nafee to come work for him but he refused, and so did Lil Smoke.

He walked in the crib and took off his sneakers.

"As-salaam-alaikum, son," Yasir's deep voice said as he came out the kitchen in his work clothes.

"Wa alaikum salaam, brother," Nafee replied with an upset face.

"You okay?"

"Nah, the job turned me down," he said, sitting down in the living room full of Islamic books and thick carpet with the strong scent of Muslim oil perfume.

"Walmart?"

"Yes, but I don't really want to talk about it."

"I understand, but I'll see you later." Yasir left the house, leaving him alone.

Nafee went upstairs to Lil Smoke's room because he hadn't been spending too much time with him since he came back from college. He opened the door without knocking to see Lil Smoke on his bed counting money. Nafee never saw so much money in his life.

"What da fuck, bruh!" Lil Smoke yelled seeing Nafee enter his room.

"May bad."

"Nigga. you supposed to knock, ask to enter, then salaam, ma nigga. You a fucking Muslim," Lil Smoke said, trying to push all the money off his bed onto the floor.

"Where you get all that from?" Nafee asked.

"All what?"

"Come on, Smoke?"

"Nigga, you a college nigga. You don't know about this street shit."

"You a school kid, too, so put me on." Nafee closed the door behind him just in case Yasir doubled back. Even though he didn't go into their rooms, he was still cautious.

"You gotta keep this shit on the low," Lil Smoke said.

"I ain't gonna tell nobody,"

"I'm robbing niggas until I find a plug so I can lock shit down with Lil Trap," Lil Smoke said.

"Lil Trap a loose cannon."

"Maybe, but bruh got a lot of love in Liberty City," Lil Smoke says about his best friend.

"Did you show him all that?" Nafee pointed at the money.

"Hell nah. I'ma wait until I find a plug, then I'ma turn him on cuz I got this, but since you down now, I'ma need you to do some shit for me," Lil Smoke said like a true boss.

"What?"

"Open up a business bank account. I want to start saving money, but before you do that, find us a two-bedroom apartment in Homestead or Carol City."

"Smart. So we don't bring dirt back home to Yasir, even though he used to be cold blooded when he was with them," Nafee said, looking at the photos of Savage and Britt.

"Facts, but this shit can get nasty," Lil Smoke warned him.

"I know."

"Okay. Good. Welcome to the family," Lil Smoke joked.

"Nigga, please." Nafee laughed it off but he knew his life was about to change.

Romell Tukes

Chapter 4
Norwood, Miami

Yasir pulled up next to Norwood Middle School for a pipe issue across the street at a gray house with a BMW truck parked in the first yard. He worked hard every day for his plumbing service. He would normally work alone, or he would bring some young Muslim brothers from Mosque fresh home from jail looking for work for extra help.

Getting older, Yasir's focus was on a better life. He'd been married for two decades to his beautiful wife Hira. His wife was full Arab, mainly Afghan. Her family were from Kabul in Afghanistan. There were times where he wanted to go back to the old crazy Yasir who used to kill people for fun, but when Savage got killed, he had a new responsibility. Yasir always promised Savage and Britt that if anything were to ever happen, he would raise Lil Smoke correctly in an Islamic setting. When they died, he kept his word, but 'til this day Yasir still didn't fully know what happened at that gravesite Savage and others died at. The only news he got was there was a woman at the scene and a snake. The news reported that the woman killed four police officers and got away. Yasir knew she had to be a professional.

He grabbed his toolbox and made his way inside thinking about Nafee, hoping Allah would guide him down the right path. Raising Nafee and Lil Smoke was very easy. They were good kids, but he feared his and Savage's blood would soon start to appear.

Yasir had another son, but he died a while back due to some very serious health issues. Nafee was too young to really have a bond with his little brother because they both were babies. Losing a child crushed him and his wife. He had been seeing a lot of young kids get killed by police and from gang violence. He felt sad and prayed Nafee and Lil Smoke beat the odds.

***

Liberty City, Miami

Travis, AKA Lil Trap, got on his dirt bike and started it up, about to make his way over to 79th Street near the flea market to see his boy Bowy. He loved riding dirt bikes or motorcycles since he was a little kid. That was his shit. In his neighborhood they called the Hamps, he was well respected at age eighteen. He'd already killed a gang of niggas who had a name in the streets. Lil Trap was feared, but he knew being feared could be a downfall or an uprise. He wanted to make some big money and his hood was the goldmine. Another hood full of money was called Pork-N-Beans projects, but he had beef with the nigga who ran it by the name of Jiam because he shot his cousin.

Lil Trap's best friend Lil Smoke called him earlier, letting him know he needed to speak to him. The two friends went back to the sandbox and swings. Lil Trap used to spend the night at Yasir's crib almost every night growing up. Lil Trap was considered family. Even though he wasn't a Muslim, he still followed their house rules when he was there.

Lil Trap lived in the projects with his mom, grandma, and younger sister. His dad was in prison since he could remember, for killing a man. People in the street never really talked about his dad, more so about his late cousin Bama who terrorized the streets with a man named Savage in his crew a long time ago. When Lil Trap heard Savage was Lil Smoke's brother, he couldn't believe it. His friend had some gangsta in his bloodline.

Lil Trap only had a few hundred dollars to his name, and that wasn't how he got down, so he was going to holla at Bowy to see if he had a lick for him. Bowy was a robber. He knew everybody who was getting to a bag in da 305. He had a hit list. He and Lil Trap were from the same project and were related through marriage.

Lil Trap parked his dirt bike next to Bowy's old school donk sitting on 24-inch rims.

"You still riding dem little shits, bruh?" Bowy laughed.

"I'm not complaining but I need a lick. Shit bad right now," Lil Trap said getting off the bike.

"Rob a bank."

"Fo'real, dawg, stop playing. I know you got something in the works." Lil Trap knew how Bowy got down. He stayed busy with robbing muthafuckers.

"I did. Some nigga name Pain, but niggas ran up in his spot and fucked him over real good."

"Fuck. He would've been my moment."

"I don't know about that. His brother is KVon and that nigga connected to some big-time people who would kill everything you ever loved, bruh. Trust me. I'ma try to come up with something. Give me a few days," Bowy said, leaving him no time to reply.

Lil Trap heard of Pain before in the streets, but he couldn't remember where. He had to meet Lil Smoke at Liberty City Park right now. He always took the back blocks to avoid police, but he would put them on a chase at least twice a week. He loved the rush.

It didn't take long for him to get to the park. There were a few people there he knew but he wasn't a people person, so he paid them no mind.

"What up, bruh? I ain't see your ugly ass in like a week," Lil Smoke joked on Lil Trap as he did daily.

Lil Trap was a skinny, medium-height, handsome cat with long dreads. He had a yellow complexion and a smooth demeanor. "Shit been fucked up. I just tried to get on, but a nigga gave me the spin around."

"I thought you was selling pills or some shit?" Lil Smoke asked.

"Fuck that. I started using my own drugs to relieve stress. I'm so broke." Lil Trap laughed.

"I got something that's finna take care of all dat." Lil Smoke walked to his new car he'd just copped. He bought a four-year-old Lexus LS but it was still in good shape.

"This you, cuz?" Lil Trap asked, looking at the car he knew cost a nice penny.

"Yeah." Lil Smoke grabbed a yellow envelope full of blue faced and passed it to him, smiling.

"What's this...? Oh, shit." Lil Trap looked around as if they'd just robbed a bank.

"Chill, you good. That's all you." Lil Smoke loved to see others happy. That was his good character he got from Savage and his mom Lisa.

"How you get this and how can I get me some?" Lil Trap wanted to know because he knew Lil Smoke didn't rob or sell drugs.

"I'ma put you on soon, but lay low. I got some shit in the making. I'm just planning. About to build a team once I find a plug," Lil Smoke said.

"You find a plug?" Lil Trap was confused.

"I'll explain in a few days." Lil Smoke left.

Chapter 5
Downtown, Miami

KVon laid in bed thinking about the funeral parlar, watching the workers place a white sheet over his brother's face. This was his second time here since Pain's vicious murder. The funeral was done a few days ago so he was planning on flying the body out to Haiti to be buried. He felt like Pain's death was somewhat his fault because he brought him into the game while he laid back and tried to get legit. KVon knew now it was time to show his face and find out who did this. He was waiting on Do Do to get back to him.

Do Do was the voice of the streets and could find out who killed the president if KVon asked him. Even though he was low key, a few people still knew he was the man behind the success.

Thanks to his plug Royal, he was able to distribute all across south of Miami and Haiti. He wondered who knew Pain's every move to the tee where they were able to rob and kill him. KVon knew Pain was very smart with his dealings and the way he moved. One thing KVon knew for a fact was everything done in the dark will always eventually be brought to life.

***

Bulawayo, Zimbabwe

Umar loved the good African food his maid would cook for him on a daily basis. His mansion sat on fourteen acres near the city of Bulawayo. This was one of his homes he came to in the times of meditation. Umar's younger daughter was in the other section of the mansion with her friends. She was really getting on his nerves, but she was his baby girl. Tonight, his other daughter, Khadija, was on her way because he had something to tell her. He found it amazing how after all these years she still looked the same as she did when she was a kid.

He was still one of the biggest drug dealers in Africa. He used Khadija as his enforcer and muscle. Growing up he found it odd for him to picture himself being one of the biggest drug lords in the world.

When Khadija told him she killed Savage he felt as if that was the wrong idea. It was too soon. Umer knew Savage and his crew could muscle him a ton of money. He knew she always completed her contracts and Savage was on her list; it was personal and business for her. Umer heard his daughter's voice and called her name out loud.

"As-salaam-alaikum, father."

"Wa-alaikum salaam," Umer said as he looked at his daughter, not liking what he saw. She was dressed in casual clothes with Chanel signs all over her outfit, but the open-toe heels is what caught his eyes. Umer was used to Muslim women covering themselves in garments and hijabs, especially his daughters. "Why are you dressed like this?" He asked in his African accent.

"I'm grown now."

"You are still a Muslim," he shouted. This was one reason he never wanted his kids to go to the United States and get brainwashed into their negative affairs.

"I know, dad, and I still do what I'm supposed to do as a Muslim woman," she shot back.

"Except cover yourself so men won't lust for you," he spat back

"I didn't come here to argue. I came to see my brothers and sister." She started to get frustrated.

"Okay, well, we have a problem on our hands," Umer stated seriously.

"What now?"

"You forgot something," he said.

"Who, me?"

"Yes, Khadija. You left Savage's son behind."

"Savage's son?" This was Khadija's first time hearing this.

"He had a son or little brother he left behind."

"How do you know this?" She asked because she didn't remember him having a child.

"I have my sources just like you have your little cyber hacker friend who hacks into my personal accounts." Umer smiled, getting up and walking closer to her.

"You have a lot of snake ways, my father."

"Where you think you get your ways from now? If I was you, I would clean up this little mess and come outta retirement. Enjoy your weekend. And one of your brothers died. He disobeyed me." Umer gave her a stern look before walking off.

She thought hard about what Umer had just told her but it wasn't adding up to her.

Romell Tukes

Chapter 6
Mexico City, Mexico

Royal lit a cigar and blew it out slowly, looking at his sixty acres of land in front of his house. The mansion was 29,692 square-feet outside the Mexico City area. His uncle Mantanta left him in power before he got killed, but Montanta also left his empire with his daughter Alina. Not too many people knew Montanta had another nephew and a daughter.

Royal was a part of the Mexican Cartel, but he had plans of moving to Miami soon and opening up with a woman named JNYX who was a man named Jo Jo's ex-wife. Relocating right now to Miami was the best thing because two big cartel families were at war and he was caught in the middle.

His wife and daughter were in the house asleep, and he was about to wake them for breakfast the maids were making. Since Alina was in college at the University of Miami, he had time to run shit how he liked to run shit. Moving to Miami was good so he could keep an eye on his little cousin.

Royal always thought about the beef between Montanta and Goya and the Savage crew in Miami. Flaco and Chulu were close to him before they were killed; he had love for them. If Savage wasn't already dead then Royal would've did it himself. Running a cartel was more so like a job to Royal. Since a kid in Mexico, he had a vicious, violent side, but he also had a soft heart for kids and women, unlike other cartel families.

Royal was a handsome young man in his early 30's with a beautiful wife who used to be Ms. Mexico.

Guards surrounded his land at all times just in case a situation popped up because he was into it with a lot of other cartel families over the Gulf of Mexico where he was transporting drugs through the border with the help of Border Patrol. Moving to Miami would be his best bet right now. He already spoke to his wife about it and she loved the city of Miami. He knew it wouldn't be hard to muscle his way into other cities when you had good product.

***

Little Havana, Miami

Lil Smoke came out to Little Havana to find a plug with Lil Trap whose friend knew somebody who had keys for the low. "This the block?" Lil Smoke asked, driving down Lafett Street off Main Street where Cubans were scattered throughout the neighborhood.

"Yeah, I think it's down this alleyway." Lil Trap pointed down a thin alley.

"Iight, but this shit looks dead out here," Lil Smoke said, feeling as if something was off about this whole scene.

"Let me call Four." Lil Trap called his boy whose plug he was coming to see. When Lil Trap got the voicemail, he hung up.

"How well can you trust this Four cat?" Lil Smoke asked, seeing the alley was a dead-end.

"What the fuck?" Lil Trap yelled, seeing seven Cuban men come out from behind walls with AR15 assault rifles.

"We got set up." Lil Smoke tucked a brown bag full of money he had in his lap under his seat.

The car was now surrounded when they saw a Spanish man with no shirt on and two gold chains around his neck approach. "Get the fuck out the car." The man opened the driver's door.

"What the fuck is this?" Lil Trap asked keeping his hand close to his hip where his gun was.

"Four robbed my little brother and you're his people, so I'm gettin' back what's mine," the Cuban man said with his goons behind him. The man's name was Hero. He controlled a block in Little Havana but he had keys of dope at a low price. The only thing about Hero's product was it was taking drug users' lives because he was cutting it wrong.

"That ain't got shit to do with us, bruh," Lil Smoke spoke up.

Hero got close in Lil Smoke's face, taking the toothpick out his mouth. "Sorry, my boy, but around here we tic for tac."

Car headlights came speeding down the alley. There were six all-black GMC trucks driving towards the men. Hero focused on the trucks, wondering what was going on. Seconds later, armed men stepped out with the biggest military rifle Hero ever saw in his life. When Hero saw Mucho get out, his heart began to race like a rap beat.

Mucho approached Hero and slapped him so hard blood started to leak from his mouth. "Go," Mucho told Hero who worked for him.

"Sorry, boss," Hero said before leaving.

When Hero and his men left, Mucho looked at Lil Smoke and Lil Trap. "Follow me and I'll fill y'all in when we get to my house." Mucho walked off and climbed in his truck, pulling off.

Lil Smoke looked at Lil Trap and did what Mucho said, but Lil Smoke had a feeling Mucho was somebody big. At the same time there was something strange going on and Lil Smoke nor Lil Trap wasn't feeling it.

Romell Tukes

Chapter 7
Miami Beach, FL

Mucho pulled into the gated, long narrow driveway filled with all types of luxury cars and motorcycles. His home was 26,541 square feet with five bedrooms, three bathrooms with glass showers, two walk-in closets, four-car garage, and a large basement with an inside bar.

Mucho is Papi Goya's son he kept on the low to save his life and protect him from the dangerous game. Now since Goya was gone, he took over his drug operations with the help of his stepsister, Lura, who shared the same dad but different mothers. Months ago, Lura told Mucho about a letter she had from her dad, Papi Goya, saying for them to look after Lil Smoke. It wasn't hard for them to find Lil Smoke, especially when Mucho found out he killed Pain.

Pain and Mucho had a relationship in the side hustle. Mucho was providing Pain with drugs on the side as well as his brother KVon. Pain wanted extra money, so he started making side deals with Mucho.

Walking into the house, Lil Smoke and Lil Trap both looked confused as to what was going on. Mucho's goons walked off to another section of the house.

"Have a seat. Y'all drink?" Mucho asked.

"Nah, we good, but what's going on? We ain't even know that dude," Lil Smoke said in their defense.

Mucho laughed before sitting down on his $200,000 couch, grabbing a piece of paper off the table. "No need to be worried, but I want you to read this and you'll have a clear understanding of me," Mucho said, looking in Lil Smoke's green eyes, passing him the note.

Lil Smoke read the note out loud so Lil Trap could hear. "Dear Son, and to my dear step-daughter, by the time you have found this, I'll be dead, but I know I went out like a true OG as this generation says. Savage is a special friend of mine, but at this moment I don't think he'll be alive either by the time you get this. I want you and

Lura to take over my empire. I have everything in order for you both. When Savage's little brother gets older, I want you to find him and bring him into the family with open arms. His name is Lil Smoke … I love y'all." Lil Smoke could tell the letter was old, but it sounded legit to him.

"That's my dad, and he vouched for you, and that's rare. Come out to the back so I can speak to you in private for a second. No disrespect to you, Lil Trap. Give us a second," Mucho stated.

"You know my name," Lil Trap said happily.

"I know a lot." Mucho and Lil Smoke got up and walked out back.

Out back, Mucho had a large jacuzzi and two gazebos near the courtyard.

"My brother must've been a likable guy," Lil Smoke said, walking down a walkway.

"Not really, but my father used to speak highly of him to others, so that's a good look," Mucho said.

"Okay, so who are you and how did you find me?"

"My stepsister found you, but she's in London right now."

"Okay, what's this about?" Lil Smoke asked.

"I know you robbed Pain, and KVon gonna be looking for you. That means Royal will be looking for you also," Mucho told him.

"Fuck it."

"Your right, but you can't go to war with no money."

"I got a little money," Lil Smoke added.

"You got shoe money, but I'ma show you how to get real money," Mucho said, stopping.

"Real money?"

"I don't like repeating myself, but I'm a connect, Lil Smoke. I'm sure you noticed that already."

"I'm just trying to make some real money," Lil Smoke said.

"I'ma get you to a level you need to be in life if you let me."

"I need a plug," Lil Smoke stated.

"You got one now, but I have a few demands," Mucho said.

"What?"

"First, never rat. Second, never play with my money. Never, cross me. Stay loyal to me and I'ma stay loyal to you," Mucho said.

"That's all?"

"Yes, and you need to form a team and try to take over South Miami. That's my goal. it's a lot of money and competition out there."

"I'ma work on that. Give me a few weeks," Lil Smoke said.

"Okay, but just to welcome you to the family, I have a bag for you and Lil Trap."

"Thanks."

"Watch your back. I meet up with you in a few weeks. I'ma have my men take your number."

"Okay, we locked in." Lil Smoke shook Mucho's hand, about to enter a new life.

Romell Tukes

Chapter 8
Key West, FL

Jnyx had a private gym in her glass house mansion in the lower section of her home. Exercising was a big part of her daily lifestyle. At thirty-two years old she still looked as if she was in her early 20's because she took good care of herself and she was strict on what she consumed into her body. Jnyx was a beautiful woman—cocoa brown complexion, medium height, bright hazel eyes, perfect smile, medium length curly hair, and she was thick in all the right places. She looked like she could be on a reality TV show.

A lot of people knew her as Jo Jo's wife or one of the biggest dope dealers in the 305. When Jo Jo was alive, they got married in Mexico while he was running a cartel out there. Getting married was the happiest part of her life because she came from nothing. Growing up in Carol City, Miami had its ups and downs in her life. She lost her brother to the streets and three uncles to the game she was now playing.

Marrying Jo Jo was the joy of her life; no man ever treated her with so much love and care. When she met Jo Jo she was a young girl working in the KOD strip club, shaking her ass to make a living until Jo Jo took her out of the club and showed her a boss bitch life. The night Jo Jo was killed in the warehouse, he told her he was going to see his sister Britt's husband Savage. Getting the call from the hospital about her husband's death that night was always re-lived.

She knew Savage killed Jo Jo. She was happy when his death surfaced but she wished it could've been her to kill him. One thing she didn't understand about Jo Jo's and Savage's death was how at both of their crime scenes there was the same type of snake left behind.

Jynx's sister Solana lived with her when she wasn't at school. Her sister, nineteen and beautiful, Jynx wanted to find a better life. Her sister didn't know about Jynx's life because she kept it so secret from her.

Jo Jo left her a couple of million dollars and her little sister knew that, but Jo Jo also left her tons of kilo's and she didn't look back since. Miami had a lot of king and queen pins, but she wanted to be number one. She wanted to lock down the whole tri-county area from Miami, Broward, and Palm Beach. Jynx had been dealing with the Mexican Cartel, but for the past two months or so the product had been weak and she didn't want that on her name at all.

After her hour workout she went to take a bath and ate a healthy meal to get ready for the day.

***

Downtown, Miami

Khadija drove to the airport to pick up her little sister who called her a few days ago informing her about an issue she had back home in Africa. Her little sister Emma told her about how their dad was tripping and bugging on her. Khadija knew her sister was still a teenager, and at the point of her life she felt like she knew everything.

Having a father like Umer had its pros and cons. The good to it was he was rich, so whatever they wanted they had. The side effect was he was a very strict father because he followed the Islamic religion.

Growing up, Khadija couldn't even have friends, but he lightened up on Emma because she could have friends over and go out at times. She knew Umer had a quick temper if one of his children didn't follow his rules or obey his strict orders.

The news of Savage having a little brother fucked her head up. She knew in a matter of time if she didn't get a hold of him, he could become a big issue. Once she got her little sister settled, she planned to do some research into Savage's little brother. Khadija was heavy on tying loose ends with any killing she ever did.

She slowly pulled up to the entrance of the airport looking for Emma. Within a couple of seconds, she saw her. Emma was dark skinned with long hair down to her ass. Her beauty was out of this world. She was perfect. She had hips, curves, a fat ass, and the perfect height. Emma wore low cut jeans showing her flat stomach and a Louis Vuitton tank top holding her small titties. In Africa, the dress she was wearing was a sign of disrespect to their families and religion.

"Look at you," Khadija said, getting out of the car.

"Hey," Emma said with her head down.

Khadija knew something was wrong with her sister and when she lifted her head she saw why. Emma had two black eyes and a swollen right cheek. "What the hell happen to you?"

"Me and daddy got into a big disagreement, and the next thing I remember, he was on top of me, beating on me," Emma said with tears in her eyes.

"It's okay. You're good now," Khadija said, hugging Emma. Khadija had been through the same story many times and she knew how her little sister was feeling.

"Thanks, but I'm never going back there. I'd rather be broke and poor," Emma said.

"Allah will provide for us. Come on. Let's go get something to eat." Khadija helped her sister put her bags in the car.

Romell Tukes

Chapter 9
Miami, FL

The Mint Club on 27th Avenue was packed tonight, and everybody came out to see a few rappers hit the stage and perform. Lil Smoke called his crew out so they could talk about the new power moves he came up with. Since meeting with Mucho, he'd been plotting to open up shop in Dade County where all the money was. Lil Trap and Nafee both entered his section to see two bottles of Ace and Dusse sitting in an ice bucket.

"What's going on?" Nafee asked, seeing the bottles on the table. He wore an Islamic garment in the club with the Kufi on, smelling like Muslim oil.

"As-salaam-alaikum," Lil Smoke replied, greeting Nafee the correct way because Lil Trap wasn't a Muslim.

"Wa-alaikum salaam." Nafee sat down, seeing people stare at him awkwardly.

Lil Trap tried his hardest not to laugh at Lil Smoke's brother.

"Good looking for that paper you gave me. I bought a new car and all types of shit." Lil Trap was speaking about the money Mucho gave them as a gift.

"We about to be on," Lil Smoke said over the loud music.

"What you mean?" Nafee looked lost as to what they were talking about.

"We about to take over, bruh, and I want you to be down with us just like we spoke about," Lil Smoke reminded Nafee.

"I told you I'm down. When do we start?" Nafee asked.

"Soon. I just need you and Lil Trap to get a crew rounded up of solid niggas we can trust to get money," Lil Smoke said

"I know the right people." Lil Trap knew a lot of dope boys in the city and he was going to slide on a few of them so they could get some real money now.

"Iight, I'ma go let Mucho know we ready," Lil Smoke stated.

"What will I be doing?" Nafee asked, not really knowing his position.

"I got something special for you," Lil Smoke said.

"I think we about to be like Savage and his crew back in the day," Lil Trap joked.

"Nah, I think we finna be bigger than them, cuz." Lil Smoke knew all he had to do was link up with a few dope boys in Dade County and cut them a good price on dope and coke.

Nafee tried to focus on the convo but he saw a sexy dark skin woman by the bar, and he made his way to her section without excusing himself.

"Damn, he thirsty," Lil Trap said.

"He like a little kid in a candy store," Lil Smoke said

"Can we trust him?"

"Can you trust me?" Lil Smoke asked.

"Enough said, bruh-bruh. I got you," Lil Trap said, taking a whole bottle of Ace to the head.

They both thought about how shit was about to be.

***

North Shore, Miami

Yasir got off work to see his wife in the kitchen cooking and cleaning. Everything she did, she looked sexy.

"As-salam-alaikum," she greeted her husband she loved dearly.

"Wa' alaikum salaam, baby. How was your trip back home?" Yasir asked, walking into the kitchen.

"Alright, I guess. I just wish you was there with me," Hira said.

"Next time."

"I believe you." She kissed him, missing his touch.

Hira was a classy woman from the Middle East, raised in Florida, but she was still raised by strict, old fashion Islamic parents. She had a lot of family in the Middle East so she was back and forth a lot. Hira sold clothes, make-up, and other female items online. She had her own online shop that was very successful.

"You cooking my favorite?" Yasir saw her baking fish and stew.

"Yes."

"Good. I'm striving." Yasir went into the freezer for something cold to drink.

"Where are the kids?" Hira asked because when she came back from her trip hours ago, the house was empty.

"I don't know. They getting older now. I ain't seen them since yesterday evening," Yasir said.

"We gotta keep a better eye on them, baby. You know the bloodline they both came from," Hira said, knowing about Savage and Yasir'a father who was a cold stone killer.

"You right."

"I know, sweetheart. Now, go wash your hands so we can eat," Hira told him, knowing he'd just gotten off work.

"Okay." Yasir went upstairs thinking about Savage and how he was a madman when he was alive.

Romell Tukes

Chapter 10
Tijuana, Mexican

Jynx was popping up on her plug to speak to him about the prices on the product. She also wanted to speak on the low quality of the coke she'd been getting lately because the work was getting stepped on. By the time she got the product in her hand there was no need for her men to cut it to stretch it. She honestly felt like he was trying to get over on her because she was a female in the game. Today she planned to make it clear to him that either he was going to give her the purest coke or she would cut him off.

Pulling into the real estate she saw two SUVs parked out front with other luxury cars. The home laid on the desert outside of the city of Tijuana, known for its high drug traffic. Getting out the truck she had two men with her, armed and dangerous. Jynx flew private every time which made it easy to travel with weapons. She loved her handgun she carried everywhere with her.

Jynx saw the front door was cracked, which was odd because normally Colon's guards would be at the front door on post. "Be on point," she told her crew, pulling out her weapon after she saw a man's foot sticking out behind the door. Stepping further into the house, she saw dead bodies all over the place and they were mostly Colon's men she recognized. "Y'all go search for the drugs," Jynx said, seeing Colon's dead body slumped at the bottom of his staircase with a sniper assault rifle in his hand. She could tell who run up in there meant business because Colon had ten bullet holes in his face. "Damn." Jynx made her way to the kitchen with her gun out and ready to go. She saw two dead maids with handguns in their hands. Searching the house for a few more minutes, she found nothing to pipoint who did this, but she really didn't give two fucks.

"Boss lady, we got a few duffle bags he had in a safe inside his wine room," one of her guards stated.

"Good. Let's get the fuck outta here before some cartel family connects me to this shit," Jynx said, following her men out the house with two bags in both of their hands. Jynx wasn't dumb. She knew it had to be another cartel family who killed Colon because he had strong connections. So, whoever killed him had to have some strong ties also.

***

Miami Beach, FL

Lura climbed out of her Audi two-door coupe with her laptop, rushing inside the mansion. She had to change into her work-out clothes and meet up with her personal trainer, Mell. Lura was twenty years old and alluring. She stood 5'6", long blonde and goldish hair to match her light skin tone, she was fit and slim, feisty, sexy, and very smart.

Before a well-known drug lord named Papi Goya was murdered, he had a son, Mucho, he left behind and a daughter with a beautiful black woman. Papi Goya named his daughter Lura and kept her on the low to save her and her mother from his bad lifestyle.

Lura's mother was killed in a robbery days after Goya'a murder. Lura never knew she had a brother until her mom's funeral, and he took her in and basically raised her. Mucho never knew Lura was a borderline genius until she graduated high school at fifteen years old. Lura also was a mastermind in the streets. She really was the one running Mucho's drug enterprise.

"Lura!" Mucho yelled.

"What, Mucho? I have to go. My personal trainer's waiting on me," she yelled, trying to rush to her room but he popped out the kitchen, seeing her Muscle Gang fitness gear.

"It's gonna be fast," Mucho said walking by his goons.

"Damn. What, bro?"

"Since when exercising became more important than your brother?" He asked.

"It's not that. You know how I hate to be late for shi,t" she shot back.

"I found that Lil Smoke kid. I brought him into the family. I want you to meet him soon."

"I will."

"When? I barely see you, Lura. If you not at your condo or traveling, I never see you," he said.

"Mucho, unlike you, I have friends and a life." She knew Mucho's life was business.

"I'm not gonna argue with you. Call me."

"I will." She ran to get her gym bag so she could meet her trainer then go to eat with a few of her friends, so she had another outfit to change into inside of her Nike gym bag.

Lura's room was large with its own walk-in master bathroom and closet. It looked like an apartment.

Chapter 11
Downtown, Miami

KVon drove the Wraith through the litty Miami streets, passing luxury cars left and right. He was on his way to meet up with Jiam at a nightclub to tell him about the nigga who killed Pain. The past few weeks KVon had been trying to find out who the kid in the footage was that killed his brother. He knew Jiam knew everybody in the city that was somebody.

KVon parked and went into the pool hall which had a bar inside. The spot was full of Cuban women. As he looked around, it wasn't hard for him to notice Jiam because he was the only black dude in the spot. "Jiam, good to see you." KVon gave Jiam a firm handshake. KVon always looked classy in suits and designer gear; the type of shit white men wore on Wall Street.

"How you doing, big homie?" Jiam shot back.

"I'm trying maintain, but we need to talk." KVon sat down, digging in his pockets for a photo he printed out of the person who killed and robbed Pain.

"I'm all ears," Jiam said, sucking on his gold teeth.

"This kid killed my brother and I want him dead." KVon handed Jiam the picture, seeing him look at it hard and long. "Do Do helped him obtain the footage of the whole scene at the restaurant the night Pain was killed."

"I don't know him. He looks young, bruh," Jiam stated, handing KVon back the photo.

"I know, but I need you to put the word out I want this nigga dead," KVon told him.

"I got you."

"I hope so." KVon got up to leave the pool hall.

Jiam stared at the picture, trying to memorize the face. He planned to ask around to see if niggas knew the little nigga.

***

Miami University, FL

Lil Smoke had a homeboy in college he knew since he was a kid his named Ronny. The two kept in touch daily. Yesterday, Ronny inboxed Lil Smoke on Facebook, telling him to come out to his party he was having on campus at his dorm. Lil Trap wanted to come out to just to get away from the hood.

"I got a few meetings set up with some big dawgs from all over the city, bro." Lil Trap rolled up a blunt of weed.

"Aiight. I hope you not smoking that shit in my new car." Lil Smoke had just bought a new big body BMW, all-black, with tints and a system inside.

"I know you don't fuck with this type of shit, but where we finna park at?" Lil Trap asked, seeing it was a full lot.

"It's a spot right there," Lil Smoke said, seeing an empty space. He parked and they made their way into the dorm area.

Loud music could be heard coming from the dorm unit Ronny told him to come to.

"Damn, this shit live," Lil Trap said, seeing all types of beautiful women from all different races coming in and out the party, having fun.

"Facts, bruh." Lil Smoke walked into the big apartment, seeing people bunched up drinking and smoking. He saw Ronny standing next to the DJ booth. Ronny was 6'4" and a basketball player for the school. He was the school jock so he would throw parties and everybody would come out, especially the women. "Ronny!" Lil Smoke yelled, getting his bo'sy attention while Lil Tap already had a chick on the wall, dancing on him.

"Smoke!" Ronny gave Smoke a bear hug.

"What's up? This shit turned up," Lil Smoke said, looking around, seeing one chick who caught his eye. He saw a sexy Hispanic chick in a lime green dress in the kitchen with a gang of chicks laughing. They made eye contact and Ronny peeped the vibe.

"I see you brought crazy Lil Trap with you." Ronny and Lil Trap didn't have the type of friendship Lil Smoke and he had. Lil Trap disliked Ronny because he wasn't a street nigga and he saw him run from a fist fight in school, so he thought Ronny was pussy.

"Yeah, that's the bro regardless of what you two have," Lil Smoke said while catching the chick in the lime green dress stare at him.

"You like what you see?" Ronny asked.

"Who is she?" Lil Smoke asked.

"That's Alina. She a classy chick. Everybody be on her but she not going at all. I never saw her on nobody like this, bruh," Ronny said in Lil Smoke's ear because the music was so loud.

Lil Smoke saw her leaving and there was no way he was about to let her walk out without him shooting his shot. "I'll be back," Lil Smoke said, seeing her leave, following her. Outside there was a big crowd of people but he didn't see the chick in the lime green dress. He finally saw her on her way to the parking lot. "Alina!" he yelled out, seeing the woman stop.

"Do I know you?" She turned to look at him, not recognizing him from around campus.

"No, but I saw you inside and I just want to try to get to know you. I know niggas be on you all day, but I know you felt that connection," he said, making her smile.

"What's your name and why I never see you on campus? It's only but so big," Alina said.

"I'm Lil Smoke."

"Lil Smoke, huh? That's not your birth name," she said.

"Go out with me on a date first and I'll let you know," he said, looking into her green eyes and her pretty face.

"Okay. Take my number and call me. I have to go back to my dorm to get some rest."

Lil Smoke took her number and went back into the party, asking Ronny about Alina's background.

Romell Tukes

Chapter 12
Little Havana, Miami

Hero loved his neighborhood because nothing went in or out without him knowing. Today was his little brother's twenty-first birthday. He walked into his aunty's rundown crib in the hood to pick up his brother to take him out.

His little brother was handicapped in a wheelchair, so Hero had to treat him with special care. A van full of shooters waited on him because there was some beef going on with the Zoe Pound nigga. Hero had been having issues with the Zoe Pound for a few months now, after two of his spots got robbed by them. Having a plug like Mucho he could flood the whole Miami, but the only problem was he disliked the way he treated him. Last night, Hero met up with another plug and tried to make side deals.

"Come on, Andre," Hero told his little brother who was sitting in front of the TV watching cartoons while his aunty was sleep in the back. Hero rolled his little brother outside, singing Happy Birthday to him in Spanish. When he got to the sidewalk, he saw two gunmen with Dracos rush him and one approached the van.

Tat, Tat, Tat, Tat, Tat, Tat, Tat, Tat …

"Remember me," Lil Smoke asked as Hero watched Nafee kill his goons.

Hero froze with the wheelchair handles in his hands as his little brother drooled on the pavement. "Mucho sent you?"

"Smart man," Lil Trap stated.

Before Hero replied, Lil Smoke and Lil Trap filled his body with bullets from their Dracos. Lil Smoke saw Hero's little brother and shot him twice in the face, showing no type of remorse.

The crew rushed to their stolen Honda truck and pulled off.

***

Downtown, Miami

Mall of America was packed today with shoppers from all over. Khadija gave Emma a few stacks to go shopping in the mall. Emma was loving Miami. She had never been. She'd been to the West Coast and to New York a few times but that was about it.

Being born and raised in Africa into an Islamic background her life only limited her to so much. Seeing sexy men with big muscles, tattoos, and women barely naked was new to her. Growing up under a father like Umer, she had to learn the whole Noble Quran before she even knew what a textbook was. Emma was gifted; she spoke different languages, a skilled fighter and shooter like her older sister, but she didn't like violence. Her English was so good nobody would believe she was from the motherland.

Getting away from Umer felt so good she finally felt free after 20 years. Emma wanted to find a career now. She loved designing clothes, so Khadija mentioned opening a clothing shop somewhere in Miami. Since being in the 305, she'd been coming across a lot of men, but one of them grabbed her full attention a few days ago in a club. Going clubbing was cool. She had a lot of fun. She wasn't a drinker, but she'd been sipping here and there. When she met the man of her dreams, the two vibed all night. The man's name was Nafee, and when she found out he was a Muslim her pussy got drenched.

Emma never felt so comfortable with another male as she did with Nafee. They only hung out once, but tonight they had a date, so she was looking for something sexy to wear. It took her five hours to shop and pick something out for later. Nafee haven't left her mind since she saw his sexy ass.

***

North Miami, FL

Nafee felt like a goofy taking a chick to a Cracker Barrel restaurant but he wasn't used to this and he didn't want to do too much on their first date. Emma seemed like a very simple girl. When he met her at the club they clicked and talked all night. He felt a vibe with her not only because she was a dime piece, but because she was a Muslim. Finding a good Muslim woman was hard nowadays so he felt like he lucked up. He'd been thinking about Emma since the first time he laid eyes on her sexy ass.

Nafee sat at a table waiting for her to arrive. He had flowers for her. When he saw her walk in rocking a dress and heels with her hair flat-ironed, he felt his dick wake up. She had hips and thighs with no stomach. He couldn't believe he bagged her because if he didn't know her, he would assume she was an Instagram model.

"Hey beautiful," Nafee said, handing her the flowers, standing up.

"As-salaam-alaikum, first," she said as she smelled the flowers.

"Sorry … Wa-alaikum salaam." Nafee forgot whenever a Muslim saw another Muslim it was best to greet them first.

"So, let's eat," Emma said, sitting down on the chair he pulled out for her.

"You look good." Nafee looked at her dark smooth skin he loved.

"I try, but you look fresh. What do you do for a living? I forgot to ask you that on the phone" She was getting a lot of attention from lookers.

"I just graduated college so now I'm looking for work."

"Work?"

"A job," he corrected.

"Oh, okay, cool."

"How about you?" He asked.

"I want to be a clothes designer and open up my own clothing store," she said proudly.

"Oh, yeah. I think Miami is a good place."

"Me, too," she said.

They talked for hours, having a good date, and made plans for another one.

Romell Tukes

Chapter 13
North Philly, PA

Umer landed at a private strip with his private jet. He came out to see one of his wives and his two children he had with a woman he married six years ago.

Umer had a few Muslim brothers he sold drugs to. Delaing with Americans was very iffy because there was a lot of snitching going on. In Africa he had the government and law enforcement in his pocket, so he basically did what he wanted.

Since Emma left, he'd been stress-free. He didn't have patience for his daughter who wanted to disobey Islam and his own rules. He knew the only place she would go to was Miami with her sister. Plus, Khadija called him, telling him she was with her.

When Umer got the news of Savage having a son or little brother, he knew it could turn into a big problem if he didn't fix it now. He knew Khadija wanted to retire and live a regular life, but he knew in reality that would never be able to happen. Khadija was his personal assassin and whenever he needed some serious work done, he would manipulate her or force her by death. Umer was so vicious, one time he used Emma as bait for Khadija to go and kill one of his rivals. He told Khadija if she didn't kill him, then he would kill Emma, and he meant every word of his threat.

Umer had a crib in Philly, so he took an Uber to his wife's crib to spend the week with his family. After Philly, he had to go to New York City so he could check on his workers. Umer had a crew of Africans in BK getting money with the dope he was shipping them.

***

Miami Hospital, Miami

Mrs. Akbar was the wife of one of the most known doctors in the city of Miami— Dr. Akbar. She was a Muslim woman form Morocco and was beautiful. Working at the hospital over two decades, she was ready to retire in five years from now. Her and her husband had a beautiful daughter in med school.

"Dr. Akbar, your working late tonight?" An older white woman asked, approaching one of the ICU rooms where Dr. Akbar was checking up on a patient.

"No. Why'd you ask?"

"It's about to be shift change."

"Oh gosh. I have to get home." Dr. Akbar took off her gloves, scrubs, and lab coat, leaving her hijab covering her face.

"Have a good night!" The white lady really liked her. She'd never been around Muslim woman until she met Dr. Akbar and she was impressed.

Dr. Akbar left the hospital and drove home in her Porsche coupe, knowing her husband was waiting on her as he did every night. She decided to use the highway instead of the main streets to get to Miami Beach— the rich section of the city. The highway was empty so this made it easy for her. While driving she saw a pair of headlights in her rearview mirror on her bumper.

"What the hell?" she asked, coming up on an exit.

The four-door large pickup truck rammed into the small Porsche, making it slam into a line of water bins. Dr. Akbar crashed, almost killing herself as the airbags blew up in her face. The pickup truck pulled up behind her on the empty expressway and a woman in all-black rushed out with a gun in hand.

Dr. Akbar was conscious, so when the door flew open, she was able to realize she was at gunpoint.

"Can you hear me clearly?" Khadija asked.

"Yess… ohhhh …" Dr. Akbar felt blood dripping down her forehead into her eyes.

"Almost a decade ago there was a man named Savage. He was shot ten times and was taken to your hospital and your unit. I want to know if he survived or not," Khadija explained nervously after saying Savage's name in vain.

"I don't remember him coming to the hospital, but I heard of that name. I think he died at the scene with a snake somewhere near him." Dr. Akbar got a good look at the woman's face.

"You lying to me?" Khadija asked.

"No."

"Okay." Khadija had to hunt Dr. Akbar down because she'd been having dreams about Savage being alive and killing her. Before walking off, Khadija shot her in the head twice then got back inside her pickup truck, racing off, hoping the dream was only a dream.

Romell Tukes

Chapter 14
Miami Beach, FL

Lil Smoke got a call form Mucho last night, asking him to meet him at his home early in the morning. Lil Smoke drove in his new all-white Dodge SRT Charger Hellcat widebody to Mucho's mansion for their meeting. He wanted to bring Lil Trap along, but Mucho asked him not to. Lil Trap was in Overtown, Carol City, and Liberty City trying to gatherer up a small army of loyal niggas, trying to get some real money.

Last week he and Nafee moved into a two-bedroom apartment in Overtown. Since killing Hero, he had been feeling like this was only the start to a new life. At times Lil Smoke thought of what it was like for his brother Savage when he was running the streets with his crew. Lil Smoke looked up to his brother. Even though he was gone, his memory was still present.

Pulling up to the gates of Mucho's crib he saw all types of foreign cars out front. It took the gate a second to let hm in once he hit the buzzer. He parked next to a nice red Audi two door coupe and walked to the door.

Two big black men opened the front door with ice grills.

"We have to search you," the guard with dreads said.

"Okay." Lil Smoke left the gun in the car because he didn't take Mucho as a threat.

"Mucho will be right with you, sir. You can wait in the living room. He knows you're here," the bald head guard said after the pat down.

"Iight." Lil Smoke walked into the living room to see photos of Goya and family members. He looked out the living room window to see a woman going for a swim. He looked a little harder to see a Spanish woman do laps in the pool. The woman stepped out and climbed out the pool, dripping in water. His mouth dropped when he saw her flat stomach, nice breast, and cute face as she dried off and wrapped a towel around her waist.

The woman disappeared somewhere, and he heard someone coming down the stairs.

"Lil Smoke," Mucho said with a smile, holding a box of expensive cigars.

"Mucho, what's up? I see you brought the smoke down."

"Only the finest for you," Mucho said sitting down.

"I took care of Hero," Lil Smoke said.

"I know. That was classic. And to reward you, I want you to take over Little Havana. You will be well guarded out there."

"Okay, cool. I'm on it."

"But first, I want you to meet my partner and the person you will be dealing with most of the time when it comes to your deliveries and drop offs," Mucho told him.

"I'm putting my trust in you," Lil Smoke repeated.

"I hope so because I'm putting my trust in you. Lura!" Mucho yelled his sister's name.

"When will this first shipment be ready? I have some paper because I don't want nothing free," Lil Smoke said.

"Your money is no good here for the first delivery. I want you and your crew to keep that money and be able to feed your wolves, buy nice things, and re-up on the next round when you come back."

"I'ma have two right men I deal with— Lil Trap and Nafee."

"I deal with you, Lil Smoke. Not your crew. And if I was you, I would also keep my circle tight. Once you start seeing the type of money coming your way, you will come across hate, envy, and jealousy from those close to you. Their desires will turn into corrupt desires," Mucho said as his sister's high heels could be heard through the house.

Lil Smoke understood what his plug was saying. He was excited about finding a connect. It seemed unreal. He would always hear rappers talk about it.

"Our guest is here." Lura walked into the living room wearing a Versace outfit and heels. She looked good and Lil Smoke couldn't help but notice.

"Yes, this is our guy. I was just telling him most of the time my brilliant sister will be handling the business affairs like now because

I have a flight to Cali, so, Lura, take care of him. Lil Smoke, I'll be in touch whenever you get done with your first drop off. Welcome to the family." Mucho passed him the box of cigars before leaving with his two goons.

"I hate the smell of them shits," Lura said as she sat down, crossing her legs, looking at him up and down.

"I don't smoke."

"That's good. Well, I'm Lura, his sister. I knew you would be a good fit, but I don't like your attire, so I'ma have my designer go shopping for you," she said as he looked lost as she pulled out her phone to text her designer.

"What?"

"I don't like how you dress. You're about to enter a new lifestyle. Our appearance is everything. You're very handsome but you need style in your life, and I'ma make sure you fly." She smiled.

"What does this have to do with getting money?"

"A lot. My designer is on his way. As far as the shipment, give it four days and my people will meet you in Bunch Park." Lura went to the kitchen to grab two bottles of water.

Lil Smoke looked at her nice round ass and he could tell she did a lot of exercising. "Thanks."

"For what?"

"Finding me and trying to help me."

"These are orders from my dad and he must know you got the same bloodline as Savage." She passed him a water.

"I guess so."

They talked all day until her designer came with a van full of gear for him. Lil Smoke left looking like a million bucks.

Romell Tukes

Chapter 15
Downtown Miami, FL

Dr. Akbar's husband, also Dr. Akbar, and his beautiful daughter sat in the front row of the funeral of his wife. When Dr. Akbar got the call about her death, he was fucked up about it. He knew his wife didn't deserve to die how she did on the highway, left for dead. They were having an Islamic funeral for his wife whom he truly loved to death. His daughter rested on his shoulder, crying a river for her mom's loss.

"It's okay, baby girl," he stated.

"No, it's not," Scarlit, his daughter, said.

"Trust me, it will be, baby girl," Dr. Akbar stated seriously, wiping his daughter's tears. He couldn't figure out why someone killed his wife. It didn't make no sense to him. Today was a sad day for him, but he planned to do his own investigation on his wife's death because the police wasn't any type of help whatsoever.

***

North Miami, FL

Jnyx went out alone to get her nails and feet touched up for a big party she planned to attend. Her sister was supposed to come out to get her nails done but she changed her mind last minute. Jynx was waiting on her homegirl to come through to vibe with her.

Jnyx couldn't believe someone had killed her connect. Now she needed to find a new plug. Not too many people liked Jnyx because they knew she was the late Jo Jo's wife. Jo Jo had a lot of enemies from the shit he did, but she knew most people he had beef with were dead.

After she got her nails and toes done up, the sun was going down, but it was still hot out. Walking to her car she didn't see a gang of masked men. Before Jynx could turn around two men tackled her to the floor, tying her up, trying to toss her in the back of a truck. Jynx screamed, yelled and kicked as if she was a civilian. The men tossed her in the truck, peeling off out the parking lot.

***

Dade County, Miami

Jynx was blindfolded and dragged out to the garage area in the hood.

"Sit her in the chair," a male's voice said calmly.

Jynx was done putting up a fight. She knew it was pointless. If it was time to die, she was ready. "Fuck all of you bitches!" Jynx yelled like a mad woman.

"Take off her blindfold and I want everybody out of here," the man said.

"What the fuck do you want?" she yelled as her blindfold came off. When the blindfold dropped, she was now face to face with Royal. She thought the young Mexican man was handsome, but she knew whoever he was he had to be somebody to kidnap a woman of her status.

"Jynx, you may not know me, but I brought you here for a reason and it's not to harm you," Royal told her.

"Well, you made me break a fucking nail, asshole." She got feisty on him, making him crack a smile.

"Colon from Tijuana was your old plug, am I correct?"

"I don't know who the fuck you talking about," Jynx said, not knowing if the man was the police.

"I killed Colon and took over Tijuana. My pops used to run it until Colon took over, but I took control of it. I know he was supplying you, so I'ma give you an option," Royal said, kneeling in front of her.

"I got what option?"

"Let me supply you, or I can feed your pretty feet to my killer sharks." Royal smiled.

"What would you do with my body?" She played with his threats.

"I may keep it for myself," he said back.

"I don't even know your name, Mr. Kidnapper," she said.

"Royal."

"Royal who? Are you Montanta's son?" Jynx had heard of Royal. His name was heavy in Miami and Mexico.

"Yes."

"So, you want to team up with me?" she asked with a laugh.

"Yes."

"This is a good way of showing me you're interested in business."

"I have a weird way of doing a lot of things," Royal stated.

"I'm all in. So, when do we start?"

"Now," Royal said, getting her untied and taking her out to eat.

They talked for a few hours and she made the choice to deal with him on the business tip.

Romell Tukes

Chapter 16
Miami University, FL

Alina walked through her school's hallways texting Lil Smoke, laughing to herself at his comment he'd just texted her. They had been getting to know each other lately and she was more than delighted to take her time getting to know him as a person; something people rarely did these days.

She was staring at the text where he asked her out on a date, but she did not reply.

Alina showed a few of her homegirls pictures of Lil Smoke from his social media page and they were all cheering her on. There was something about his long hair and colorful eyes that drove her crazy.

The night she met him at Ronny's party she couldn't stop thinking about him. He gave her chills at just the thought of him. She asked Ronny about him and he only spoke good things about Lil Smoke. The night she went to the party, she wasn't about to go, but now she was glad she did. She admitted to him that she saw him first that night.

Alina made her way to her next class then she planned to meet up with her big cousin for lunch who was a nutcase, but she loved him.

***

North Miami, FL

Khadija felt like it was a nice day to attend a beach with her sister Emma, to enjoy the hot summer.

"Did you bring some sunscreen?" Emma asked in her Chanel bikini, laying on a beach towel. Emma saw a lot of males watching her because her bikini disappeared between her fat ass cheeks.

Both women laid on their stomachs, but Khadija was covered up in a garment.

"Hell nah."

"I love it out here," Emma said as she looked around the beach at the beautiful people.

"How do you like it out here?" Khadija asked.

"I love it. Especially the party scene." Emma laughed because she loved the Miami nightlife, but she wasn't a party animal.

"I barely see you," Khadija stated.

"Lately I been spending a lot of time with this dude I told you about."

"What's his name again?"

"Nafee. He's real cool. I want you to meet him soon," Emma said, looking at her for her stamp of approval.

"Soon, but I just want to make sure you are serious with him first, little sis," Khadija stated.

"I feel you," she replied, looking at a dark-skinned brother with a six pack on a jet ski.

"He's too old for you," Khadija said as she saw Emma looking at an older, handsome male.

"You looking, too." Emma laughed hard because her sister played militant but she was a freak just like her on the low.

"I'm older."

"No, you need a man," Emma joked, forgetting her husband was murdered but she had no idea Khadija murdered her own husband.

"I'll be okay," Khadija said sadly, trying not to think about Bama, her late husband. She loved Bama, and at times she regretted killing him, but she had to live up to her contract.

***

South, Miami

Myalessa worked in the clinic in Liberty City. She was Lil Trap's sister and was beautiful but hood. In half an hour she was about to get off and get up with her boyfriend Trigs. She had been with Trigs for years but their relationship was going downhill slowly but shortly. Lil Trap had been calling her all day for her birthday but she was busy.

Today she turned twenty-one years old and was living alone with her man, but she really wanted to get out of the city. Her boyfriend was selling drugs for a big-time drug dealer named KVon for a few months now. Myalessa didn't want him selling drugs at all; she knew the outcome could be death or jail. She was scared her for little brother who was running the street crazy.

She clocked out five minutes early and texted Trig to see where he was because he picked her up every day from work because he didn't work.

Leaving work at seven at night, it was dark outside, but she saw Trig's luxury car parked there on time. She smiled, ready to give her boo some head for him being a good boyfriend. "Babe!" she screamed, happy to see him as he got out of the car.

"You ready," he asked, seeing a Maybach pull up with tints that looked familiar.

"Who dat?" Maylessa asked.

"My peoples," Trig said as he wondered what his plug was doing here out of all places.

"That's a nice car," Maylessa said as Trig went to the car window to see KVon behind the tints.

"What's going on, boss man?" Trig asked as KVon got out of the car.

"That's Lil Trap sister?" KVon asked, staring at Maylessa's thickness and her pretty face.

"Yeah. Why you ask?" Trig saw something in KVon's face.

KVon pulled out a gun and shot his worker in the neck. Maylessa was so shocked she didn't know whether to run or scream as she froze.

Boc ...Boc ... Boc ... Boc ... Boc ...

KVon shot Maylessa in her chest, watching her body collapse before walking off, hoping Lil Trap would get his message.

Romell Tukes

Chapter 17
Downtown, Miami

Nafee took Emma out to a season one hotel which had its own jacuzzi in the room.

"Tonight was so fun, Nafee," Emma said, sitting between his legs, relaxed. She loved the way his body felt, and she could feel his big cock threw his shorts, but she played it off.

"I really like you, Emma, and I'm trying to lock you down," Nafee said as she turned to face him.

"You sure?" She looked surprised

"Hell yeah."

"I want you to, baby," Emma replied, making her juicy lips meet his as their tongues filled each other's mouths.

Nafee's hands worked her perky breast and suddenly he pulled off her top, and she wriggled out her panties as he did the same. He began sucking on her super sensitive tits, making her wetter. Emma felt her moisture trickling down her thighs into the warm jacuzzi water. She couldn't wait anymore.

"Fuck all dat foreplay, Nafee. Just fuck me!" she screamed as she reached down and grabbed his big penis, knowing he was about to fill her up.

Nafee slowly thrust his manhood into her as she yawled with pleasure, holding on to the edge of the jacuzzi.

She rolled her hips on each downstroke, making him touch all the spots that needed to be touched. "Ohhhh, yess! Fuck me, pleaseee!" she yelled, cumming. Her pussy muscles squeezed and milked his cock as he came with her, emptying his liquid into her good pussy.

Emma turned and bent over, exposing her big, round ass cheeks. He entered her gushy love box from behind, making her leap forward.

"Shit!" she screamed, biting her lip.

Her wetness and tightness sent pleasures rocketing through his body as he picked up his rhythm pumping in and out of her. Emma's screams got louder as they echoed through the site, but this made him thrust harder and harder until she came again.

They got out of the jacuzzi, went to the bedroom, and made love on the mattress and fucked like two crazy people.

***

Carol City, Miami

The news of Lil Trap's sister's death had him going crazy for a week straight, but now he calmed down as he attended Myaleessa's wake at his aunty's crib in Carol City. Lil Trap sat in the kitchen, looking at the bottle of liquor he was drinking as family members flooded the crib saddened by her death. Nobody would ever think Myalessa would've died the way she did in the streets by a gun, but everybody thought she got killed because of Trig who survived the shooting.

Her family disliked Trig because of what he was into. They knew Myalessa was a good girl and Trig was toxic. Lil Trap knew Trig worked for a man named KVon and he knew that was Pain's brother, so he had a feeling the murder wasn't about Myalessa.

"You good, bruh?" Lil Smoke wore a nice outfit to pay his respect to Myalessa, his boy's older sister. Since kids, Lil Smoke always had a crush on Myalessa and everybody knew it, but she used to think it was cute but never pursued it because of Lil Trap.

"I'm straight dawg."

"You sure?" Lil Smoke knew when he was down.

"You remember that time we went to that car show at South Beach when we was fourteen and Myalessa got into a fight with that light skin chick who had all that acne on her face?" Lil Trap asked, thinking back. People walked in and out the kitchen, grieving.

"Yeah, nigga. How could I forget? We got jumped by ten dudes form Overtown that day." Lil Smoke laughed, sitting down.

"Yeah, you did your thing that day, you feel me? But the crazy shit... I saw that same bitch Myalessa beat up last year and she remembered me."

"Oh, shit. What she say?"

"I fucked her the same night, and her shit was on point. Shawty head game was on another level." Lil Trap laughed for the first time since his sister's death.

"You crazy, but it's time. We got the product and goons. Now let's put this shit into motion."

"I want KVon."

"You think he did this?"

"I know he did, bruh. I can feel it, dawg," Lil Trap said upset.

"Iight. Let's put a plan together," Lil Smoke said as Lil Trap's aunty called him in the living room.

Romell Tukes

Chapter 18
North Miami

Royal was glad he had a chick like Jynx on his team because he knew her resume and he was more than happy to join forces. Today was Royal's and his beautiful wife Sonnia's birthday. She turned thirty years old but looked like a teenager still.

Sonnia was pure Mexican from Mexico City, and her family was super rich, so the lifestyle Royal gave her was nothing new.

They went out to a Spanish food spot owned by Sonnia's uncle and ordered dinners.

"How was vacation, baby?" Royal asked, thinking about how good she looked today with her hair in a Chinese bun.

"Good. I just wish you would've come with me but I'm glad to be back." She blushed.

"Me, too." Royal saw his two guards patrolling the area outside.

"I have something I need to tell you," she said seriously.

"What could that be, birthday girl? Please tell me," Royal says, loving when his wife got serious. He remembered the time he fell in love with her. It was love at first sight. Her beauty could be detected out of the biggest room.

"I'm pregnant." Her words sounded like an echo in his ears.

"Excuse me," Royal said.

"I'm pregnant, stupido." She caught an attitude because she didn't like his reply to her pregnancy.

"I'm sorry. I'm just overwhelmed." Royal was honest with her.

"Overwhelmed?" Sonnia was about to go in on him because she was a very feisty chick. Before she could completely go in on him, gunfire erupted, shattering the windows.

Royal threw Sonnia on the floor next to him while covering her.

Tat … Tat … Tat … Tat … Tat …

Close to about fifty rounds tore through the restaurant, hitting five people.

"Come on, follow me," Royal said as he grabbed her arms and drug her to the back exit.

Once they got the back, he saw one of the shooters sneaking his way inside through the back exit door. The shooter was on his tippy toes.

Royal saw the man through the mirror in the corner ceiling. He pulled out his gun and fired two bullets into the man's upper torso, making him drop his SK assault rifle.

"Ahhhhhh!" The gunman yelled in pain on the floor while bleeding heavily.

When he looked back, he thought he was tripping. He got her off the floor and rushed her out back, hoping the wound wasn't serious where she could die. Royal made it out back to see a few SUVs pulling off. He knew they were Mucho's goons who just bought the attempt on his life. He took his car to the nearest hospital, trying to save his wife who was unconscious.

**

Palm Beach county, Miami

Mucho drove on the highway in a large Suburban truck with dark tints and security. The truck was doing eighty miles per hour as he was on his way home. Mucho sent his goons on a mission to take out Royal and his wife. He knew Sonnia's family owned a restaurant and she went there every first Saturday of the month. He was waiting on the call now to hear the good news about his number one rival's death.

The beef between him and Royal was before their time, dealing with Papi Goya and Montanta. He knew Royal was doing big things in Mexico and certain areas of Texas. He knew Royal was trying to take over Miami on some sneak shit and he refused to let that happen. He had enough people to worry about.

Mucho's phone rung two times and he picked it up with a smile. After a few seconds of talking, he hung up and banged on the dashboard. His goons told him they didn't know if Royal was dead or not. Mucho gave clear direct orders to run up in the spot and shoot Royal and his wife in the head. There was no doubt that Royal would put two and two together and figure out he sent the hit because nobody else would have the balls to do it. Maybe Jinx or a crew looking for a come up. That's why he sent Lil Smoke and Lil Trap on the hit with a few of his men but told them to play the background.

Romell Tukes

Chapter 19
Brooklyn, NY

Umer came out to Red Hook in Brooklyn for an emergency meeting with his workers who were mainly Africans and West Indians, locking down Brooklyn and other boroughs.

Leaving his family in Philly was always hard but all of Umer's baby mothers knew his lifestyle. He was in and out, but he did take care of all his kids.

The dark skies always gave New York a deadly look but Umer was used to death. Since Emma went with Khadija, his home in Africa had been more than peaceful.

"We're here, boss," one of Umer's guards said as they pulled into a warehouse parking lot surrounded by eight-teen wheelers trucks.

"This shit better be good." Umer got out and walked to the crowd of people looking for Dontea, his cousin from the Motherland but he had been living in Brooklyn for twenty-two years.

"Umer, we got a problem," Dontea said, coming out from inside an old broken-down warehouse used to store fish and meat products.

"I don't like problems," Umer replied

"When the truck arrived, three of my men were dead and all the shit was gone," Dontea said.

"You're telling me you let my shit get robbed." Umer felt his anger raise.

"Well, basically."

"Where was the truck driver? He had to be on your payroll?" Umer asked with his strong African accent.

"The driver said he made three truck stops but have saw nothing out of the ordinary or noticeable that stood out."

"Okay."

"How can seven hundred bricks of Heroin just magically disappear? I think there is a little more to this and if I find out –" Umer couldn't finish his ideal threat because shots rang out and Dontea's head popped off like zit.

Tat, Tat, Tat, Tat, Tat, Tat, Tat, Tat, Tat …

Umer ran back to his SUV while his men covered him, trying to see where the bullets were coming from.

Bloc, Bloc, Bloc, Bloc, Bloc …

The warehouse turned into a big shoot out as everybody from Umer's crew and Dontea's crew aimed at the roofs where they assumed they mayhem was coming from.

"Fuck that. Come on, let's go." Umer yelled out of the bullet-proof truck window.

Umer feared the unknown and not being able to see who was trying to kill him made his heart race.

One thing he knew for a fact is whoever was shooting at him had to be an elite shooter the way Dontea's head busted open.

Umer couldn't think straight as the trucks got on the Brooklyn bridge heading to New Jersey where he had a condo.

He had a lot of enemies but not in New York. Dontea couldn't have set him up because he was the first to die. Umer tried to think of anything and everything he could to put the pieces to this puzzle together, but it wasn't adding up.

The only person he could think of who had a shot like that was his daughter, Khadija.

***

Jackson Memorial Hospital, Miami

"You okay, baby?" Royal asked as he stood over Sonnia, seeing she was much better than his last visit here to her.

"I can't believe I pulled through," Sonnia stated with a raspy voice because the shot to the neck grazed one of her glands, but the doctor said Sonnia would be good.

"You're a soldier."

"You saved me." She smiled.

"We got a new crib so when you leave here, I am settled in our new home. Trust me, you're going to love it," he told her.

"Where?"

"Key West. Your mom designed it floor to wall."

"My mom here?" Sonnia knew if her mom would see her like this she would have to hear about this forever.

Sonnia's mom disliked Royal, but she would put on a fake smile for her daughter's sake.

"Yes, I told her what happened, and I flew her out, but she is awaiting your arrival any day now," Royal stated.

"When will I be able to leave here, baby? I'm sick of eating dry food and animal crackers." Sonnia made her husband laugh because he knew how spoiled she was and how Sonnia had no choice but to eat the hospital food or she would starve.

"In three days, they told me."

"Okay, I guess."

"First day out, how about we go out the states?"

"Shopping spree?"

"Whatever you want, baby." Royal felt like it was his fault she was even laying in a hospital bed and breathing heavily.

"I love you."

"Love you too. I'll be back tomorrow. The guards will be outside if you need anything. I have to go to Mexico."

"Be safe!" She yelled out as loud as she could before the door closed.

Royal nodded to the guards in the hallway, who were causing a lot of attention.

"Sir, you can't have these many visitors," a male nurse said, approaching them.

"Shut the fuck up and start feeding my wife some real food. Better yet, I'ma having my people drop her off food," Royal demanded, scaring the shit out of the nurse as he wished he would've minded his business.

"Yes sir." The nurse walked the opposite way, trying to hold his legs as tight together as possible feeling the warm urine slid down his legs.

"Half stay here and look over Sonnia while the rest come with me," Royal told his twelve man crew.

Royal had to go have a meeting in Mexico with some Cartel families about future business plans. He recently killed one of the main suppliers and a lot of families wasn't feeling that, but luckily, Royal had a few plans up his sleeve to make everybody happy.

***

Sawgrass Mall, Miami

Lil Trap took Bowy out to the biggest mall in the city of Miami in Broward County.

"I can't believe niggas killed cuzzy," Bowy said, referring to Myalessa.

"Don't remind me." Lil Trap parked the Lexus next to an all-white Audi R8 Spyder causing both to stare at it, climbing out of the car.

"We finna slide on dem niggas, cuz." Bowy always was ready to lay some shit down.

"This going to take time. It's bigger than why you think bruh, feel me?"

"Well, my niggas ready."

"All I need you to do is keep providing shooters and workers because me and Lil Smoke about to take over Miami. At least, Dade County. On everything." Lil Trap added, walking inside the mall to get him and Bowy some gear.

"I told you the gang on deck, cuz. We all trying to get to a bag. We may be young and wild but we about da paper, ya feel me," Bowy said, looking forward to getting rich with his cousin.

"Tonight, we supposed to get our first load so when I call you be ready." Lil Trap walked into one of the stores, looking at all of the designer shit he had been seeing Lil Smoke wearing.

Lil Smoke told him Lura took him shopping because she disliked the way he dressed. Now, Lil Smoke was on some fly boy shit.

"Do you think Lil Smoke really built for this shit?" Bowy asked not really knowing Lil Smoke as well, only seeing him a few times here and there.

"Bro, Lil Smoke in rare form. He really a monster cuz. Let's say he got a two sided demon in him." Lil Trap laughed, seeing a cute, dark skinned dime piece chatting with some bozo looking nigga wearing a suit.

"Peep dis shit," Lil Trap said, making his way over to the woman he couldn't keep his eyes off.

"Ms., I think you lost something," Lil Trap said, interrupting their conversation, saving the day.

"Me?" She asked checking inside her Louis Vuitton purse.

"You lost my soul because when I laid eyes on you, I lost all of me." Lil Trap saw her smile shine bright.

"Aye, how about you take that corny ass game over there?" The man she was talking to said

"How about you kick rocks before we kick your ass?" Bowy said, popping up and the man got ghost.

"Oh my God. You saved the day. He was so fucking annoying and thirsty," she said looking at Lil Trap and how cute he was.

"I'm Lil Trap."

"I'm Solana but I like your little game. I can't front. That was a real vibe," Solana told him as they walked around the store.

Solana was eye candy. Medium height, long dreads, petite body frame, chinky eyes, and flawless dark skin.

"I had to say something, feel me. Win, lose, or draw." He admits as Bowy was picking out so many outfits the store employees was watching him and thinking he was stealing.

"You won with that big energy, but you may want to keep an eye out on that dude who you pushed away. He may spin the block on us." Solana had a sense of humor with beauty.

They walked around the mall for two hours after he gave Bowy a few bands so he could do him.

"I don't want today to end. You're so crazy." She laughed as he helped her with a couple of bags.

Lil Trap opened every door for her like a true gentleman and she was digging that a lot.

"We can link up again."

"I be so busy with school that I don't have time for myself," she explained.

"I understand."

"But my girl is having a birthday in Club Live next week." She gave him a look to see if he was down.

"I'm there, can I bring the gang?" He asked.

"Okay, why not but my girls are super boujee." She admitted.

"We just coming to have a good time."

"Cool, you got my number, use it. Bye, Bowy." She waved at Bowy who placed the bags in the Lexus.

"Nice car." Lil Trap saw her climbing into the Audi.

"On this ain't nothing."

"I hear you, boss don."

"Boy stop. Call me." she pulled off.

"You really got her number. She on a different level. She bad," Bowy said seeing Lil Trap watch the Audi drive away. He was not hearing a word Bowy was talking.

Chapter 20
Palm Beach County, Miami

Yasir drove his work truck to a job he had to do near a parking lot and run down football field.

For the last two weeks, he had been jammed pack with jobs all over the Tri-County. Getting sleep felt like a gift nowadays. Even if he wanted to take a long nap, somebody would call for his service.

Since Nafee and Lil Smoke moved out, shit been too quiet around the house. Truth be told, him and Hira missed the kids.

Real life was serious and Yasir didn't think either one of them were ready for what was ahead of them.

Looking at the clipboard for the correct address, he saw the nice house in front of him was his customer's right address.

Yasir grabbed his tools while looking at the nice car parked out front. When he walked to the door, he knocked twice and heard a female respond.

"Plumbing," Yasir yelled, hoping the customer's kitchen leak wasn't that bad.

A woman wearing a facemask to clean her pores and hair curls opened the door. Yasir stared at the woman for a second because she looked awfully familiar, but it was hard to get a good view of her face.

"You're here, come in," Khadija said, opening the door and trying to see where she saw him before, but it wasn't adding up.

"Nice place." Yasir saw a lot of Islamic things like prayer rugs and photos of the Kaba, which is a prayer temple located in the middle east.

"Thank you. I like the area, but the problem is right here." Khadija showed him to the kitchen and opened the sink lower cabinet.

"A leak," Yasir said.

"Yes, it's been like this for two days," she said as Yasir quickly found the issue.

"You have a cracked knob here, but I have a new piece right here." Yasir dug in his bag and pulled out a small metal piece.

"Thank you so much."

Yasir unscrewed the sink and easily replaced the broken piece with a new piece.

"If you have any more problems out of this, please let me know." Yasir got off the floor, looking at her perfect toned body.

"Do you take cash or credit card?" Khadija grabbed her purse off the kitchen table.

"You're fine. No need. That only took a second of my time. You're okay," Yasir told her.

"Thank you, have a good day." Khadija let him out.

"Question, do I know you?" Yasir had to ask the question that had been on his mind.

"Not that I know of."

"Okay sorry."

"It's cool, enjoy your evening and thank you again." Khadija looked at Yasir awkwardly as he walked outside, feeling like she crossed paths with him more than once.

Yasir got inside his truck and drove off, changing his thoughts to something else forgetting about lady sink he had just fixed. He didn't have a clue that she was the one who murdered his boys Bama and Savage.

***

Bunch Park, Miami
Later that night

"Nobody in here bruh. Are you sure she said come out here?" Lil Trap asked inside the driver seat of his car.

"Bruh, it just hit 7:30pm. Chill out, dawg. You making me uneasy," Lil Smoke told him as he waited on the first shipment.

"What's happened with da Lil Havana shit, bruh? I spoke to Bowy, and he didn't mind going out there," Lil Trap said.

"Nah I'ma open shop out there just in case something goes wrong. Plus, I'ma need you to have them in Liberty City, Carol City, Lil Haiti, and Robin Hood. Then, once we lock down them hoods, we focus on Palm Beach and Broward County. Feel me?" Lil Smoke knew with patience he could really control the streets.

"Nigga this ain't the BMF. We got real competition out here folk."

"I know that, and I got a plan for that." Lil Smoke added.

"Let me hear this."

"Either they eat with us or eat dirt cuz. Period."

"So, we kill every plug?"

"Yep."

"We don't even know if we'll have that much product to feed the city bruh." Lil Trap made a clear point.

"We shall find out tonight," Lil Smoke repeated before the tap at the window scared them both.

"What the fuck?" Lil Trap was about to shoot Lura for creeping up on them like that.

"Damn, Lura." Lil Smoke got out.

"Y'all real jumpy but I've been watching you two for five minutes. Safety precautions, you understand. You never can be too safe," Lura said, dressed in running gear.

"I hear all dat," Lil Smoke replied.

"Hey Travis," Lura called Lil Trap out by his real name. He was wondering how the fuck did she know his government?

"I see you did your research." Lil Smoke added.

"Yes, on you, Nafee, and Travis but take a walk so I can explain to you what's about to happen," she said.

"Thanks for hooking me up with all that gear the other day. You dropped like forty thousand on me," Lil Smoke said rocking the Amiri outfit she got him.

"Yes."

"When you drive off, my men will follow you to wherever but this ain't no field trip. Don't have my people riding around with two hundred keys. Get them to a good location and they got you," Lura said.

"Did you just say two hundred keys?" Lil Smoke thought he overheard something.

"Yes, and that's on the house. Me and my brother's gift to you." She gave him a warm smile.

"Wow, I don't even know what to say."

"Don't say shit, get money. Your brother was like family to my dad, and I loved my dad. If he says you family, then it's that. We don't fuck with too many people at all, but we do got beef. Real beef," she told him.

"If you got beef, then so do I."

"That sounds cute, but I got to go to the gym and tone up. Them muscle gang fitness dudes looking like they came out Dr. Miami office," she said.

"Do your thang."

"Call me when you done and be safe, but most of all smart."

"Facts."

"Bye." Lura jogged off up the block, placing her iPod in her ear and heading to the nearby gym.

Lil Smoke couldn't believe he was about to touch two hundred keys. He thought she was going to send ten to twenty keys at most.

"What that sexy bitch say?" Lil Trap asked when he got in the car.

"It's two hundred joints in that van for us."

"Hold up bruh. Two hundred bricks?"

"Yeah."

"Ain't no fucking way, cuz."

"I put that on everything. We got to take it to my crib until we find somewhere to stash it." Lil Smoke pulled off.

"We finna be super rich." Lil Trap saw big dollar signs in his eyes as he danced his money dance in the car seat. Lil Smoke laugh before they played some Kodak Black.

Chapter 21
Overtown, Miami

"We can't keep all this shit here. This shit looks like you robbed the plug. How did you get all this shit? Is it even real," Nafee complained as Lil Smoke and Lil Trap laid everything out on the living room floor.

"Nigga, will you shut the fuck up?" Lil Trap said tired of hearing him talk about nothing.

"You shut up." Nafee got aggressive.

"Or what nigga?" Lil Trap rushed to Nafee, but Lil Smoke got between the two men. Lil Trap was his best friend and Nafee is his brother from another mother.

"Chill out. Y'all fools want to D up, go out back. We got two hundred keys to focus on and you two niggas on some goofy shit," Lil Smoke said as both men parted.

"This a lot of shit," Lil Trap said feeling like he was in a Scarface movie.

"All this from that connect dude?" Nafee asked.

"Yeah, and we can't fuck this up. They gave us all this on the arm so that we can get on our feet. No matter what, we always pay off the plug," Lil Smoke said touching the fluffy keys.

"Hold on, this shit for free?" Nafee asked.

"Yeah, somewhat but I'ma find a way to repay him for all of this because ain't shit free in this game." Lil Smoke still felt like there was something to this whole deal. He knew his brother Savage was respected and loved but this was a lot of love.

"I wonder who that dude was in the restaurant that Mucho sent us to shoot at," Lil Trap said.

"I don't know but we was there for backup. Whoever it was must be somebody but fuck all that, we need to figure this out. I'ma put up fifty for a rainy day." Lil Smoke counted out fifty bricks and placed them in three rows to the side.

"How much a key go for?" Nafee asked, not knowing anything about the price of drugs.

"I heard them Cubans sell them to blacks for thirty-five a joint," Lil Trap shot back.

"Thirty-five dollars." Nafee was shocked but when he saw Lil Smoke and Lil Trap laugh, he knew it had to be a joke.

"No, thirty-five thousand bruh. We going to sell keys for thirty thousand but if we bust them down, we will see a lot more money. Especially, if it's some fire, feel me." Lil Smoke made it clear to them both just so there was no misunderstanding.

"I know two dudes I went to college with that dropped out of school and selling weight in Broward County." Nafee added, checking his watch because the evening prayer time was about to come in.

"Good. Go holla at them and see what's happening," Lil Smoke told him.

"I'ma take fifty to Lil Havana. Trap, you take fifty to your people, but spoon feed them." Lil Smoke counted out fifty for Lil Trap.

"Shit I'ma spoon feed niggas away but I'ma hide the rest at my aunty house. She won't mind," Lil Trap stated.

"I think I know a place where we can hide the rest of this stuff," Nafee said.

"You do?" Lil Smoke been thinking of a good spot, but he came up with nothing.

"My dad shed. We can put it in there," Nafee said.

"I don't know." Lil Smoke feared Yasir would find it.

"He never uses that thing, trust me." Nafee stood up so he could go pray in the back room.

"Okay bet, but it's on you if anything goes wrong," Lil Smoke told him.

"Cool, I ain't tripping cuz but you trying to go pray?" Nafee asked, walking in the kitchen to wudu in the sink, which consisted of him washing his face, arms, head, ears, and feet before every prayer.

"Hold on … Trap, you good?" Lil Smoke asked as Lil Trap placed fifty keys in a shopping bag.

"Facts. I'ma push up on Bowy right now and hit him with ten."
Lil Trap knew his little cousin was about to turn up in the streets
once he get his hands on this.

"Aight, hit me later bruh." Lil Smoke went to the bathroom to
do wudu and pray with Nafee.

***

Liberty City, Miami

Lil Trap left his aunty house from dropping off forty keys. He
had a place in the bathroom ceiling that he used to hide his guns.

Bowy and a gang of young niggas were all on the block in front
of a building that was known for violence and drug selling.

"Bowy!" Lil Trap yelled, getting out of the car waving his
cousin over. Bowy stopped his conversation with the gang.

"What's happening cuz? I ain't know you was coming through
tonight," Bowy said because normally Lil Trap would text before
popping up on him.

"You ready?"

"Oh, fuck yeah." Bowy got hyped already knowing what he was
talking about.

"Where you finna hide this shit at bruh?"

"I got two spots."

"It's a bag in the truck for you. It's ten keys. I want you to break
it all down fifty fifty."

"That's real bruh. I won't let you down. My little niggas ready
to turn up the street," Bowy said.

"Facts."

"Oh, I forgot tell you that nigga Trig just got out the hospital. I
heard he at his sister's house in Lake Lucerne. She dances at G5,"
Bowy said as Lil Trap popped his truck.

"I know who you talking about, and I suppose to bury Myalessa
tomorrow."

"I heard but you want me to slide over there with you?" Bowy
asked, taking the bag full of keys out the trunk before closing it.

"Nah, I got it. I'm not trying score bruh and trying to get a clear understanding of what happened. Feel me."

"Aight."

"Holla at me when you done and move smooth bruh. We on a bag now. Fuck all that dumb shit," Lil Trap told him before getting in the car driving off with Trig on his mind.

***

Lake Lucerne, Miami

Trig was laying up in his sister's apartment, still healing from being shot up by his own boss, KVon. Never in a million years did he expect for the man who showed him the game, try to take his life.

Since being out the hospital, he reached out to a few of his old friends who told him KVon put 100,000 bounty on his head for sleeping with the enemy.

At first Trig was confused to why KVon wanted him dead because he never fucked a enemy. When he heard Myalessa little brother killed Pain or had something to do with his death, he then understood.

He knew his life was in danger. The only places he could lay low was at is his sister's crib or his brother's home all the way in New Jersey.

Someone knocked at the door, and he struggled to get up.

Upon opening his sister's door, a gun was pointed directly at Trig's face.

"Go inside." Lil Trap words were cold and meant business. Trig didn't hesitate to follow the direct order.

Lil Trap saw an AK-47 and an AR-8 assault rifle on the living floor with boxes of blunts everywhere.

"Lil Trap?"

"Nigga you know who the fuck I am." Lil Trap made Trig sit on the kitchen floor.

"Look bruh, I know."

"Stop. Let me ask the questions because depending on how you answer will be the outcome of if you live or not," Lil Trap said.

"Oh, man. Please, I ain't do shit bruh. You got to believe me. I loved your sister." He cried.

"Who did it?"

"My ex-boss, KVon. I worked for him and Jiam for a few years."

"Shit," Lil Trap said very formal with Jiam. He was a little older, but they hated each other.

"Why?"

"Why what?"

"Nigga, why the fuck they kill my sister?"

"They say you killed KVon's brother, Pain or had something to do with it," Trig said

"How did they know where to find y'all?"

"Man, I don't know."

"Where can I find him all of them?" Lil Trap asked.

"Tomorrow Jiam is going to the car show downtown and Do Do always got to Club CoCo's on Tuesday."

"What about KVon?"

"He's hard to locate because nobody knows where he lives but I do know he got a 13 year old son that plays football," Trig admitted.

"That's all?"

"Yeah, I swear on my mama but them niggas ain't nothing to fuck with."

"Neither am I," Lil Trap said, lifting his weapon.

Bloc … Bloc … Bloc … Bloc … Bloc … Bloc …

Lil Trap shot him in the head and walked out on a new mission.

Romell Tukes

Chapter 22
Wynwood, Miami

Today was Lil Trap's sister's funeral and few people came out, mainly family and friends. Lil Smoke and Nafee played the background while they let Lil Trap grieve in peace.

"He good?" Nafee asked Lil Smoke as they leaned on this Hellcat, watching the crowd of people clear out except for Lil Trap.

"I hope so but losing family is the hardest feeling a person can deal with. When I lost my mom at birth, I really didn't feel anything because I had no connection to her or my dad who was killed the same day. But when I lost my brother and his wife, Britt that shit crushed me," Lil Smoke admitted.

"How do you live with that?" Nafee asked, never losing anybody he was close to besides his real mom.

"Man, it's hard. I still feel like crying sometimes but the crazy shit that fucks with me is I don't know how he really died. I heard the police killed him, then I heard some crazy bitch. I heard his best friend. I even heard it was a snake bite," Lil Smoke stated.

"Damn, I remember losing my real mom, but I was so young. Hira been in my life so long I call her mom." Nafee added as Lil Trap made his way towards them.

"There's going to be a car show tonight and I'm sliding," Lil Trap told them both, walking to his Lexus not saying another word. Lil Smoke and Nafee looked at each other already knowing it was about to be a long night in the city.

***

Downtown, Miami

Later that night at the Dolphins Stadium, the car show was big. People from all over the state of Florida came out with their cars or just to enjoy the show.

Lil Trap, Lil Smoke, and Nafee snuck in through the backdoor with their guns because security in the stadium was tight tonight.

"I see them near the old school Chevy by the stage," Lil Trap stated, looking through the crowds of people.

"What you want to do, cuz?" Lil Smoke said before two beautiful women approached them.

"Lil Trap?" Solana said, approaching him with a nice huge with Jynx by her side.

"Hey Solana, how you been?" Lil Trap looked at both women and how beautiful they were. Even Lil Smoke and Nafee stared.

"Why haven't you called me in a few days?" She asked, seeing Lil Trap attention was focused on someone or something else that wasn't her.

"I'm sorry I've been going thru some thangs," Lil Trap said.

"Okay, well call me later I guess." Solana walked off sadly.

"Damn, she's bad. They both sexy. Where you meet her?" Nafee asked.

"It don't matter. Put y'all hoodie on and stick to the plan," Lil Trap said walking around the crowds of people.

***

Jiam and a few of his boys loved cars so they would come out to every car event to purchase the flyest whips.

"I like that old school donk over there. Let's go check out the price on this bitch," Jiam said wondering if Do Do was coming out to enjoy the car show and all the sexy ladies coming out and showing lots of skin.

Boc, Boc, Boc, Boc ... BOOM, BOOM, BOOM ... Bloc, Bloc ...

Jiam saw police enter the stadium, so he creeped out with the crowd after seeing four of his goons dead on the floor. He was holding his arm while looking out for the shooters and making it outside.

***

"Oh my God." Solana got in her sister's car as people ran around the parking lot in a crisis. Everyone was scared after the shooting inside.

"Your good?" Jynx asked, seeming very calm as she got in the driver seat. She placed a gun from out of her purse under her seat.

"Yes, I'm fine but where did you get that?" Solana asked.

"I got my gun license now to protect us. Did you see them people kill all of them dudes back there?" Jynx replied.

"Who didn't?" Solana couldn't believe her eyes when she saw it was Lil Trap who killed two of them dudes.

Solana knew something was up with Lil Trap because they talked on the phone and Facetimed each other all day until recently. She found that odd. The whole time inside the stadium she watched his every move because he was acting funny. Solana thought he had a girlfriend in there or something. When she saw him shoot them two dudes, her heart stopped before taking off running with Jynx who had to grab her up.

"You hungry?"

"You seem real calm." Solana's heart was still racing at a rapid speed.

"Girl, that's regular shit. When I used to be with Jo Jo, I saw that type of shit daily." Jynx drove to a fast food drive thru, thinking how did Solana know the gunmen?

***

Overtown, Miami

The ride back to Lil Smoke and Nafee's crib was silent as everybody played in their own thoughts about what just took place minutes ago.

"How the fuck did you miss that shot?" Lil Trap asked Nafee as they stopped at a red light.

"He hit him though cuz," Lil Smoke stated texting Alina, setting up a dinner date for tomorrow at Dave N Busters.

"I just started this shooting shit. Sorry I'm not a born gangster like you," says Nafee.

"Y'all think anybody knew it was us?' I mean the hoodies were cool, but I think we should've did ski masks bruh." Lil Smoke parked outside of their crib.

"I think the only people who saw us was that chick talking to this fool," Nafee said as Lil Trap gave him the evil eye.

"She good bruh, trust that. She probably ain't even see us make that move." Lil Trap added, hoping Solana really didn't peep them.

"Hope not but I need a nap." Lil Smoke went inside the apartment as Nafee and Lil Trap went into the living room.

"Let me ask you something brother before I go in pray," Nafee said.

"So, you shoot niggas, then go pray?"

"Yeah, I shoot niggas up and ask for Allah forgiveness after." Nafee confirmed walking into the kitchen to see what they had to eat. He went shopping two days ago but Lil Trap was always eating up everything.

"What's your question?"

"Since we was kids, I felt like you never liked me and I don't know why," Nafee stated watching Lil Trap eye and body movement. It was something he learned from a self-help book.

"To be real, you just think you're better then all of us because you are book smart, make your five Islamic prayers, and you always try to seem too perfect." Lil Trap admitted.

"Wow, that's deep because I don't think I'm better than nobody. I have my flaws"

"Besides that, you're a cool nerd." Lil Trap joked.

"Thanks."

"Good job tonight but next time aim high not low. That should hit the target. Gunplay one o one," Lil Trap said before walking off to call Solana and see if she made it home safe.

***

Downtown Miami

Mucho called his girlfriend Preslee, who was in Mexico, as he sat in the passenger seat of his Tahoe truck on his way to pick up his mom from the airport.

"Hey Papi," Preslee answered.

"I miss you. What's been going on?"

"Same ole thing out here but when I come back, I'll fill you in," She said.

"Okay sure."

"My dad and brothers say they were all out here riding the horses." Preslee's family had 182 acres of land in Mexico filled with animals and farms.

"Tell them hi. I'm picking up my mother from the airport now. She coming in from Mexico City."

"Oh, they had an earthquake out there today, killing eight people," Preslee told him

"I'm glad she's here with me." Mucho pulled into the airport

"I'll be there in a few days. Keep her there so I can spend some time with her and Lura, okay."

"Love you baby." Mucho hung up, loving the fact he met Preslee ten years and they been lovers since. Preslee's family ran the Aires Cartel, and they controlled a lot of Mexico's drug trafficking.

Mucho saw his mom who was Papi Goya's second love until they split. Mucho's dad even killed his sister years back but he never built hatred in his heart because of that. One thing he knew about his dad was he did everything with reasons.

Mucho's mom was a pretty older woman in a sundress, looking a decade younger than she really was but she looked like her baby boy.

Two cars pulled up behind him and gunmen jumped out with MP4s weapons.

Tat, Tat, Tat, Tat, Tat, Tat, Tat, Tat, Tat, Tat, Tat, Tat, Tat, Tat, Tat, Tat …

Mucho saw over six bullets pierce his mom's upper torso before he caught two bullets to his legs. Mucho's guards jumped out shooting but was no match for the six shooters. Mucho was able to climb back into the SUV before it pulled off.

***

North Miami, FL

Lil Smoke and Alina went out to Dave N Buster's for a night of fun. They were playing the games, drinking, and living the life, enjoying each other's company. Something they both yearned for.

The late night calls and all day texting was great, but nothing could add up to being face to face.

"This is so much fun," Alina said, sitting down tired from playing all the machine games with Lil Smoke.

"I never came out here before I got to start having more fun," he said

"What do you do all day?"

"Me?"

"Yes, you silly." she laughed.

"I just be chilling."

"Chilling, okay. I know what that means but I don't judge," she told him.

"That's good to know but how come you don't got a boyfriend?"

"To be real, I don't have time. I focus on school so much there is no time," she explained.

"You made time for me?"

"You're different. I like you and the vibe I get when I talk to you, or text makes me feel good. It feels like I found my soulmate or some weird shit." She opened up to him.

"Sounds like your sprung." He joked

"Shut up … you don't feel the same?" She wanted to know because every time she thought about him, all she could think of if he was thinking about her.

"I do. Since I first saw you, Alina. You never left my eyes and to be here with you, I feel complete. Let's make it real and last forever," he said.

"You serious?" She asked as Lil Smoke reached in for a passionate kiss, tonguing her down and Alina loved it.

They spent the rest of the night together. He even spent the night in her dorm room with no sex.

Chapter 23
Liberty City, Miami

"This shit looks fire, bruh. How long you and your crew going to have these bricks?" A-Rod asked Bowy, sitting in his Donk Chevy on twenty-eight inch rims on 62nd Street.

A-Rod was a getting money nigga from Carol City who knew Bowy for years because they grew up together.

"We on for life now, bruh bruh. The gang eating," Bowy stated looking out of the window at his block flooded with fiends. They were coming from all over the city to try out the new crack.

"I'm proud of you, dawg. I remember you used to rob niggas coming out of McDonalds on 7th Ave, bruh. Shit, you even had me, and my crew scared to go up in da bitch. Feel me?" A-Rod laughed.

"Yeah, that was the old me. Now, I'm trying to run it up cousin. I'm trying take over South Miami."

"That's going to be hard bruh. That nigga KVon locking shit down. I heard he dealing with them Cartel niggas and you know they got an endless supply of this shit."

"Fuck that nigga but just drop off that one hundred fifty thousand to C.J later," Bowy said seeing his boys jump out a Cadillac on the block upset about something.

"You letting dem joints fly for thirty thousand a pop, cuz?" A-Rod asked, confused because everybody in Miami was selling keys for forty thousand. The least you could get a brick for was thirty-five thousand. A-Rod been copping grams lately because the price of coke was too much.

"Yeah, spread the word cuz. Believe that."

"Bet that up, cuz," A-Rod said starting up the loud engine as Bowy hopped out to see what the fuck was going on the block because niggas were all hyped up.

"What the fuck is going on?" Bowy asked the six niggas all standing there arguing.

"Niggas just shot up Rage in Opalocka, cuz," Tracey G said.

"When this happen? I just spoke to him?" Bowy couldn't believe it.

"That nigga Draft and Lucky did it. They talking about we couldn't' sell on KVon's turf and niggas got into a big shootout," Tracey G told everybody.

Bowy frequently heard of Lucky and Draft, but he had no clue they worked for KVon. He should've known because KVon had workers all over the city.

"When it hit dark out, be ready. We sliding on them fools. Tracey G, get a location on one of them niggas," Bowy told his boys, walking off and hoping Rage pulled through because that was his close friend.

Bowy treated his crew like a fraternity. They called each other brothers. It was over forty of them spread out in Miami, but their numbers were elevating at a hasty speed.

The feeling of acrimony and indignation filled everybody's heart because when you fucked with one of them you fucked with all of them.

***

Opalocka, Miami
Hours later

When the sun went down and the hot Miami heat died down, two Honda's crept through the Opalocka streets trying to be inconspicuous.

Bowy rode in the front seat with a Colt 45 handgun on his lap attached to a thirty round clip while everybody else in the car had choppers which was a Florida thing.

"Hello?" Bowy answered his phone to the unfamiliar number that popped on his screen.

"Is this Bowy?" An older woman's soft voice spoke into the phone.

"Yes, who dis?"

"Rage's mom. I just wanted to tell you my son ain't make it. I'm at the hospital. He was pronounced dead two minutes ago." The tears could be heard in Rage mom's voice.

"I'm so sorry. I promise I'ma make this right."

"I know Rage. He was very close to you so I thought I should let you know," she said before hanging up.

"He's dead," Bowy told everybody in the car to hear nothing but the sounds of weapons being cocked.

Hearing about Rage's death was about to spark an unruly, indomitable side of the crew and Bowy knew he wouldn't be able to do nothing about it.

***

Opalocka, Miami

Lucky was in his side bitch's apartment where he sold drugs. He was smoking a blunt, getting his dick sucked by the extra thick, cute redbone with a mean overbite.

"Mmmmmmm." Lucky moaned, watching his pole disappear down the back of her throat.

"You like when I do that nasty shit, daddy," she moaned before spitting on the tip of his penis.

"Do your thang."

"You going to buy me a new Louis Vuitton bag, right?" she asked, opening her mouth wide, bobbing her head. She was going slowly up and down his shaft, going to work.

"Whatever you want." Lucky lied, knowing he would never trick off on no woman.

Lucky worked for KVon. He had his own block in Opalocka, next to his cousin, Draft's block. Draft also worked for KVon. Earlier, he had a shootout with some little niggas and luckily, Draft was there to help. One of his workers got paralyzed.

Outside, he had three workers holding down the building until he was done. Lucky felt himself about to explode but the sounds of fire erupting made him jump up with his Balmain jeans down to his ankles. The front door got knocked in and four shooters ran up in the crib.

"Ahhhhhhh ..." The woman yelled on her knee, not perceiving what was really taking place until four bullets hit her in the upper chest.

Lucky still had his pants to his ankles, trying to cover up his manhood.

"Dis our block now cuz. You work for KVon?" Bowy asked, already knowing the answer.

"Yes man. You can have the block. Just let me go." Lucky saw Bowy's spontaneous smirk.

"Unfortunately, that's not going to happen." Bowy lifted his weapon.

Bloc, Bloc, Bloc, Bloc, Bloc, Bloc, Bloc …

"Search the crib for money and drugs. We got ten seconds," Bowy told the gang as they started flipping over the couch, looking in the bedrooms, and cabinets for anything.

Bowy took a picture of Lucky's dead body and texted it to Rage's mom saying *"you cry they all cry …"*

***

Carol City, Miami

Jiam waited for KVon to pull up in the plaza, which use to be the old flea market but now it was an empty area.

He still wore a shoulder strap from being shot that day at the car show, which was a dumb move shooting up a public place.

Jiam knew there were only a few crews in the city that moved ruthless and reckless to that nature, so he did an elimination and came out with Lil Trap, his rival.

The other kid he saw in the photos KVon showed him a while back was still a ghost to him. Lately, he been hearing about a new crew on the come up. He wondered if there were connection to Lil Trap. Jiam knew all the getting money crews and Lil Trap wasn't qualified to get money. He was a shooter.

An all-black spaceship Mercedes Benz pulled up with a truck behind it.

KVon got out dressed up like he was going to church but this was KVon's usual element.

"We got a problem," says KVon when Jiam gets out of his car.

"Tell me about it."

"What happened to you?" KVon saw his arm sling.

"You heard what happened at that car show a few days ago?"

"Yeah, that was you?"

"Some niggas got the drop on us, and I got a clue," Jiam stated.

"Lucky got killed last night."

"Your Lucky?" Jiam couldn't believe it.

"Yeah, they had a shootout with some new little niggas, and they came back later that night, killing a few of his workers. Then, taking him out," KVon said, still overwhelmed because Lucky made him a lot of money over the years.

"You found out who did it?"

"I'm hearing the kid that Lucky killed name was Rage. He was down with a little nigga they call Bowy." KVon saw Jiam face frown as if he knew him.

"He a kid from Liberty City. They got a little crew out there."

"Well, they stole a quarter mill and twenty keys from me that Lucky had in there for Draft to give him for me. They must be working for somebody. They just kids. I feel like we missing something right in front of our faces."

"Maybe it's that kid Lil Trap and the other one who killed Pain," Jiam suggested.

"Do Do found out the kid's name. He's a nobody they call him Lil Smoke. Do Do little sister knew him. She said Lil Smoke and Lil Trap are best friends. The crazy shit is I killed Lil Trap sister and Trig but for some reason he made it. Then, boom he pops up dead. Now some young punks are moving weight," KVon stated knowing it was bigger than what they both were seeing.

"I'ma look more into this shit."

"Don't sleep on them bruh because if all this shit is because of them two little niggas, they can be more dangerous than we think. Call me in a few days," KVon said before leaving.

Romell Tukes

Chapter 24
Miami Beach, Miami

Mucho rung the small bell he had in his bed for assistance. After being shot up, he tore two tendons in his legs and broke his shin bone, making it extremely hard to walk or move. He hadn't even had time to prepare his mom's funeral in a few days, but Lura was taking care of everything for him.

"I fucking swear if you ring that bell one more time, I'm going to break your fucking neck and fingers." Lura walked into the room with his lunch on a tray and pain killers.

"This is how you treat our own brother."

"I'm not your fucking maid. We have those but tomorrow will be your mom's funeral in Mexico. The goons and security team will fly you out tonight in a wheelchair," she said, placing his tray on the stand in his lap.

"I need you to stay here while I got out there. I'ma be with Preslee for a while okay," Mucho said.

"You sure?"

"Yes, I have to take care of some business anyway. Lura, it's alright."

"You think Royal did this?" She asked.

"It was his men, Lura. Nobody else would have the balls to do that," Mucho clarified.

"What do we do now?"

"Wait."

"Why? That makes us look weak." Lura grew upset because she knew if word got out that Royal killed Mucho's mom and had him shot, they would look soft. Then, other Cartel families could test them. Maybe even street thugs.

"I understand but Royal is just like Montanta. He reacts off impulse so right now he is waiting for us to bring him a move and that is the reason why we don't."

"So, your plan is to wait?" She asked.

"My plan will strike when the time is right."

"You sound like daddy." Lura laughed because Mucho always would say things how her father used to.

"Papi Goya was the best at tactics, and I learned to show people your weak side to conceal your strength. When they become blinded by the weakness, a little strength will destroy and demolish them," Mucho said.

"I'ma let you handle it the way you feel is fair but if they come my way, I'm thinking off impulse. I'm not playing cat and mice with him," Lura stated.

"Nobody knows about you, Lura. It's me that they want but how did things go with Lil Smoke? I like him."

"Everything went swell. He got a bright future, but I think his downfall will be his inner circle," Lura said

"Lil Smoke is a lot smarter than he looks. Don't let your foot off him. He got a lot of potential."

"I see that, but I have to pay the Cubans a visit and then my trip to Haiti is right after. I'll be busy this week," Lura told him.

"Thanks for holding shit down, Lura. I don't know where this family will be without you," he said.

"Don't try to butter me up."

"I'm serious."

"Call me later. The maid will take care of you until I get back loser." Lura left the room.

Mucho was grateful to have a stepsister like Lura on his team because without her, the family would be in deep water.

***

South Beach, Miami

Lil Trap hated coming out to beaches, especially on hot days like today. It was 107 degrees out but with the water waves and the breeze, it wasn't too bad.

Last night, Solana set up a lunch date on South Beach so they could talk. He been calling her a lot, but she would send him to voicemail and that was pissing Lil Trap off. He was really feeling her.

Walking through the sand in his Air Max ninety-fives, he scoped around the beach to see hundreds of people out having fun. He called her to ask where she was at, and Solana laughed, telling him right behind him.

Lil Trap looked back and Solana wearing a bikini under a large umbrella looking sexy in a pair of sunglasses. Her body was fit, titties sitting up nice, and her long dreads were in two braids.

"Hey sexy," Lil Trap said sitting in the extra flip chair she had for him.

"Nice to see you, Travis" she called him by his first name with a slight attitude.

"Why haven't you been answering for me?"

"Do you care?" She made no eye contact with him because she was upset.

"I wouldn't ask if I didn't"

"Do you like me, Travis?"

"Well, I wouldn't be here if I didn't," Lil Trap replied seeing her take off her Chanel sunglasses.

"Travis, I'm not for the games. Do you like me or not?"

"Yes, Solana. What the fuck you want me to do? Yell it into the beach?"

"Travis, I saw you shoot them people at the car show," she whispered loud enough so he could hear.

Lil Trip paused not knowing what to say or do. He did know if Solana would've told the police, most likely he would be in prison.

"Don't worry, I didn't tell nobody, and I never will. I just want to know what I'm about to get myself into. I'ma a good girl with a hidden thing for bad boys," she said.

"You sure you want this bad boy?" He asked.

"If I didn't, I wouldn't be here." She hit him back with his own comment, making them share a laugh.

"What this mean? We together now?"

"Yep, you're taken. I better not catch you with no bitch unless it's my choice." She let him know she had a thing for bad bitches.

"Deal but I need to know. Can I trust you?" He asked the only important thing to him.

"Yes."

"I'm holding you to that." He gave her a light kiss on the lips.

"You're a good kisser. I wonder what else you can do with them juicy lips?" She asked, blushing, and feeling her coochie get wet.

"You will find out real soon."

"Can't wait zaddy …"

They went to grab a few drinks from a wet bar and had a good time on South Beach, just enjoying each other's company.

***

South Miami, Miami

Tat, Tat, Tat, Tat, Tat, Tat, Tat, Tat, Tat, Tat, Tat, Tat, Tat, Tat, Tat, Tat …

Khadija fired the AR-15 assault rifle in Big Al's gun range, working on her shot. She wanted to come out and get some peace of mind because she had been stuck in the house for a few days. She lost sight of her target, Lil Smoke but she still had his photo and name.

Being so busy trying to look over her sister, she felt like she was a mommy. Emma would come in at all hours of the night which wasn't the problem. The issue was Emma didn't respect anything she asked or told her.

Today, Khadija had to be a real sister and kick Emma out. She already had a new apartment and car for Emma. Khadija had work to do on this Lil Smoke kid before time failed to be on her side.

She couldn't believe Savage had a little brother, seeing the photo of Lil Smoke. She knew he was way too old to be Savage's son because she killed him at a very young age.

Looking at the time on the wall, she knew Emma was probably outside awaiting her. Khadija texted Emma the gun range address and asked her to come ASAP.

Khadija turned in the assault rifle before looking at her score sheets, seeing she still had it and wasn't getting rusty. Khadija really missed her old life of traveling around the world, killing people; it was her way of life and now she felt lost.

Walking outside, Emma was next to her car smoking a blunt of weed. Khadija couldn't help but shake her head. Now, she understood why Umer sent her to Miami.

"You do know this is a gun range and police do come here."

"Police smoke weed too," Emma replied, still puffing on the exotic weed some chick she met got for her.

"Look Emma, this shit ain't working. You're my sister and I'ma always love you but it's too much for me. You're at an age where you need to be free." Khadija gave Emma a pair of keys to see a confused look on her face.

"You're moving out." A light smile appeared on Emma's face because Khadija lived a boring life and it annoyed her.

"No, you're moving out. The keys are for a room on Sixty second and Tenth, building one twelve."

"What?" Emma shouted, pissed off.

"I'm sorry but we like night and day."

"Now, my own sister turning on me, just like daddy."

"The keys are to your own apartment and a car. Everything is paid for two months. I'm sure you will be able to find a job since you like to party. The clubs are always hiring." Khadija got in her car, trying not to feel bad about this.

Emma didn't even say nothing else. She wiped her tears, feeling betrayed by her sister this time.

Romell Tukes

Chapter 25
Allapattah, Miami

KVon and two guards arrived in one of the most dangerous cities in Miami, a place KVon came to turn into a goldmine, and he did.

Since all the drama, he been trying to lay low and get money but that was real hard when little niggas were trying to take his spot in the game.

Not being one to slack or lack on his game, he did a little of his own research on Bowy and the Lil Trap. It was not hard at all, due to the fact they both had a little name in Miami.

Today, KVon was meeting with a cop he had on the payroll but also went to school with, named Baptista. He was a young looking Haitian man.

"Y'all wait in the truck. I'ma be out in a few," KVon said, getting out of the truck and walking into the diner at lunch time.

Looking around, it wasn't hard to spot Baptiste. He was a big, black, ugly fucker with a small scar under his left eye.

"Baptista, what's up, you big bitch," KVon said joking as they did daily.

"Fuck you, bitch. Good to see you man. You look like big money every time." Baptista gave him a stare, signaling him to pass his weekly pay.

"I respect the hustle but what do you have for me?" KVon asked, pulling out a stack of money from his waist and sliding it under the table to him.

"Thank you but I looked into this Bowy kid. He is a fucking hothead. Him and his little crew. Be careful with them please," Baptista stated.

"That's all?"

"He don't have too much family but I'm also working on the Lil Trav kid you asked about." Baptista assured him he was on his job.

"Who the fuck is Lil Trav? The kid's name is Lil Trap."

"I know it was something like that. No worries, I'm on it and my people. Trust me."

"I don't trust myself so why would I trust a cop?"

"Just saying, we friends."

"Do your job." KVon got up because he had a meeting with Royal in the next thirty minutes.

"I will always. You pay me too good not to." Baptista smiled as KVon left.

Baptista watched KVon and his goons pull off before answering his phone, which was vibrating the whole time during his talk with KVon.

"I'm waiting on you, big bruh," he said to his caller.

"Come outside," the man said on the other end of the line before hanging up.

Baptista got up looking around while stuffing the money KVon gave him in his back pockets. Outside, he saw an all-black SUV parked next to his work car. He had to bring back soon before his shift ended. He worked overnight as an undercover and by day, he was a crooked cop.

Baptista hopped in the SUV, shaking hands with the young man he recently met and just started to do business with.

"Lil Trap, good to see you. I got everything in motion for Jiam but the KVon shit going take a few," Baptista told Lil Trap.

"Aight bet. Just keep me posted and you will get your money weekly and a bonus." Lil Trap heard of Baptista through the grapevine and knew he would need him on the team.

"We good, bruh. Be safe out here."

"I'ma be safe. Trust that, dawg." Lil Trap touched the big ass gun on his lap.

"I see." Baptista got out of the SUV, smiling, and thinking how this was going to be the best payback for KVon fucking his high school sweetheart.

***

Miami International Airport, Miami

Scarlit got off her flight from New York. She was out there for a week, shopping and having fun. Something she did rarely because her life was always so busy.

Akbar should've been there by now but he wasn't. Scarlit called him as she stepped out the slide doors to feel that Miami heat.

"Dad, where you at?" She asked, hearing her father's raspy voice as if he just woke up.

"I fell asleep, baby. I'ma be there in a few," Dr. Akbar said, climbing out of bed.

"You sure? I can take an Uber, dad. Get your rest."

"No, I'm on my way."

" Okay," she stated, hanging up wishing she would've drove her car but Scarlit hated to drive.

Not eating all morning had her stomach touching. She saw a McDonald's in the terminal J section, so she made her way over there.

Once she got in the fast food spot, Scarlit saw a familiar face, but she was not sure until getting closer. She was not trying to be a creep, so she did it real low key.

"Lil Smoke?"

"Scarlit? Hey." Lil Smoke turned around to see Scarlit's beautiful exotic looks. She was the woman he thought about from time to time.

"What are you doing here?" She asked the first thing that came to her mind.

"I'm waiting on somebody." Lil Smoke lied because he was about to meet Lura there in a half an hour. She wanted to speak with him.

Lil Smoke had been moving weight extremely fast. She was surprised and proud of him.

"Oh okay."

"Where you off to?" Lil Smoke asked as the line to order food was going down.

"I just came back from New York. That was my third time there and OMG I love it up there." She bragged.

"Facts. I've heard it's expensive up there?" Lil Smoke asked.

"A little."

"One day, I'ma go and chill."

"I may come with you because I need to go back. Shit, I would go back now if it weren't for school." She sounded disappointed.

"At least you're focused out here and doing the best thing for your future. That's number one," he stated before ordering food for them both off the breakfast menu.

"How you been feeling?" She says referring to his wounds.

"I'm good, no complaints. I'm just trying to stay busy and active to keep my mind off it," he said.

"Okay that's good."

"You saved me, so I owe you a lot." He looked into her colorful eyes.

"Allah saved you, not me. I was just at the right place at the right time." She tried to assure him.

"Maybe."

"No maybe, that's a fact," she confirmed to him. They talked for twenty minutes before Dr. Akbar was outside.

Lil Smoke chilled outside with Dr. Akbar and Scarlit for a few before he slid back inside the airport to wait on Lura to arrive.

Chapter 26
Overtown, Miami

Lil Smoke and Nafee were in their new apartment. They were happy they just got their first place together. They had shit already moved in by the movers.

"Are you sure y'all can afford the rent?" The landlord asked. He was an old Indian man, smoking a cigar.

"Yes, we will be able to pay you every month, sir," Nafee said.

"Good." The landlord looked at both men.

Lil Smoke heard of the apartment from Craigslist last week and felt like it was perfect for them The location was rough, but it was still a low key area.

"You know what? How about this?" Lil Smoke pulled out a wad of money and counted out six months of rent.

"Okay, thank you. Enjoy please. You do whatever you want. This is all you," the landlord stated, leaving the apartment smiling and counting the money over and over.

"Damn bruh. I don't think you should've did that," Nafee said, not trusting the landlord. He looked like he would sell his soul for money and snitch if he saw anything out of pocket.

"We good, trust me. He about his money," says Lil Smoke.

"I ain't heard from Emma in a few days."

"Who, nigga?"

"The bitch I'm talking to right now, bruh." Nafee knew his brother's mind been all over the place since they been on the map.

"Aight but yo, Lura put me on to some shit yesterday."

"What?"

"Bitcoin. It's a trading thing. People can make up to millions and she got close to a billion dollars in that shit bro. On everything, cuz." Lil Smoke bragged as Nafee was not listening to a word that he said about the Bitcoin shit.

"That's what it is. I'ma help the movers bring this shit inside."

"I know mommy and pops is a little mad that we moved out. What you think?" Lil Smoke asked.

"Not really. I know my dad wanted to see us going on to elevate our life as young men focused on dreams." Nafee lied knowing his dad didn't like the thought of them moving out.

"Only if they knew what we was really doing."

"We both would be dead."

"True that, dawg."

"Where Lil Trap at?" Nafee asked. He hadn't seen him all day since they had been moving.

"One of the little niggas he know stole some money. He said this morning that he about to go handle that shit. It was his people," says Lil Smoke, shaking his head, hating snakes.

"Damn already." Nafee saw Emma calling his phone for the first time in some days.

"Niggas ain't grateful."

"Baby, what's wrong?" Nafee answered the phone hearing Emma cry on the other line nonstop.

Lil Smoke eavesdropped on their whole conversation, and he could tell Emma was somewhere at a hotel.

"Okay stay there. I'ma be there soon, baby," Nafee says hanging up and speeding to leave.

"You straight, bruh?"

"Emma got kicked out and stuck at a hotel."

"Shit, she good."

"Hell nah, bruh. That's my girl. I can't leave her at a hotel," Nafee said seriously frowning his face.

"What you going to do?"

"I don't know but I'll be back in a little bit, okay." Nafee rushed out, running into two movers bringing in their couch. Lil Smoke shook his head and texted Alina to see what she was doing.

***

West Flagler, Miami

Gee and Fags both loved playing the block day and night to get paper. They wanted to live a fast life. Today, the block was moving slow but they both made over two bands a piece.

"Ayo, bruh!" Gee popped the cup top, looking into the lean that he had been sipping since earlier. It was something he did daily.

"What's up? Roll up dawg. You been cuffing the weed, bruh," Fags stated, pulling out a wrap to smoke in.

When your cousin coming to bring the work bruh. We only got a quarter key left in the trap and you talking about some weed." Gee spit back.

"Nigga, KVon texted me earlier saying tomorrow we better have his money or its going to be a problem." Fags shook his head, knowing his cousin KVon didn't play about his money.

"You ain't tell him that we got half?"

"Half bro? That nigga ain't trying to hear that shit," Fags replied.

"Let's just ride on, bruh!"

"What, nigga? You buggin, cuz. We both going to be dead before the morning, nigga." Fags' gold grill shined as he spoke, seeing a man crossing the street with crackhead Blocko.

"We need to do something," Gee said, hoping he change his mind about KVon because they spend half of the re-up money in clubs and tricking on their baby mothers.

"Blocko, what's up shawty?" Fags said knowing the older man wanted forty dollars' worth of dope.

"Same thing," Blacko said, nodding off as he stood up next to a young man with a hoodie on. He was quiet.

"Who dis?" Asked Gee, looking at Blocko's friend.

"The grim reaper, bitch," The man with the hoodie on replied before Blocko pulled out a weapon and fired at both men.

Bloc... Bloc... Bloc... Bloc... Bloc...

The bullets entered Gee's and Fags' faces, killing them both. Blocko went into both men pockets, taking their money and drugs.

Bowy stood over Blocko, his uncle as he was robbing the dead men. He put two bullets in his uncle's head, letting his body collapse on top of the two men.

Romell Tukes

Chapter 27
South Miami

KVon waited for Jiam in the Blue Martini Brickell Lounge, which was a hot spot on Miami Ave with live performances by the city's hottest artists. It had a big dance floor, a large bar that served food, outdoor seating, great cocktails, and a great wine list.

Earlier, KVon's aunty called and gave him the news about cousin's death, and he was pissed off about Fags murder.

There wasn't one bit of doubt in his mind who was responsible for his cousin's death, and he needed blood now.

He didn't tell Jiam what happened yet because he didn't want to tell his boy over the phone. He was against that. Talking crazy over the phone was a big no in his book because he saw a lot of niggas go to the feds over wire taps.

He looked toward the front to see Jiam walking inside. He was rocking a red and green Gucci outfit, top and bottom.

"What's going on, bro?" Jiam pulled up on the couch.

"A lot. They got Fags last night on his block!"

"Fags?" Jiam shot back, not knowing who Fags was because he knew him by his government name.

"Nigga, Lil Eric."

"Oh, damn. They killed bruh bruh. Damn," Jiam said. He liked Lil Eric since he was a little nigga in the game.

"Yeah, so we need to do something quick because they getting too big headed now. They touching family out here."

"I am looking into it," Jiam said, already on it.

"I got this cop nigga on it, trying to make our problems go away," KVon stated, drinking a cocktail that he had been sipping on for twenty minutes.

"Who?" Jiam hated dealing with any cops.

"Baptista!"

"No way bro, not Baptista. You know how he get down." Jiam hated the cop. He didn't trust him at all. Nobody did because he was a snake.

"I understand but I do everything for a reason."

"I hope so."

"Look, I just need you to be there for me a little more and start making this body count match."

"Okay, I'm on it."

"Thank you." KVon got up to leave, hoping Jiam caught his drift.

***

Downtown, Miami

Alina and Lil Smoke both went out to Casablanca Seafood Bar & Grill to get something to eat and enjoy themselves because they both had been really busy.

"I aced my last exams, but I got one coming up next week," Alina said, looking drop dead beautiful.

"That's good. You really smart. I wish college were for me," Lil Smoke added, never really wanting to go to college but the thought of it was cool.

"You can still go."

"Nah."

"Why? You're smart and not too busy. Just try one semester," she coached, hoping he would.

"Maybe one day but not today," he joked.

"Fair, but what you been up this week? You barely texted or called me," she said.

"Busy."

"With what?"

"Life, and I just moved. Me and my brother been focused on that mainly," he told her, loving the grilled salmon he ordered.

"Okay, that's big."

"Yeah, I hate living with Nafee but he the bro."

"He's cool," she added, drinking the red wine, starting to feel a little horny.

"What you been doing in school because I haven't saw you in days?"

"School be driving me fucking crazy all day and I got these weird dudes on the same dorm as me who are white creeps," she said, shaking her head.

"You know how white boys get."

"They so annoying. I swear to God. OMG really." Alina put on her white girl voice, acting like white girls at her school.

"Sometimes, I feel like there is a lot of shit we don't know about each other and that bothers me," Lil Smoke spoke something that had been on his mind lately.

"I mean, I don't really feel the same way because we both be extremely busy at times. I try to understand," she replied, not knowing he cared so much but it made her feel good.

"We just got to spend more time with each other. I just moved so now you can come to my spot."

"Of course, and you better not have no bitches in there with your little friend or I'ma turn into the Hulk," She laughed, taking a sip of wine, and feeling it starting to kick in a little.

"I don't want that at all, trust me. How come I haven't met any of your family yet?" Lil Smoke asked to see her almost choke on her drink.

"Huh?" Alina wasn't expecting that question.

"I'm saying, I thought it would be nice to meet each other's families." He wondered why she was now acting a little odd.

"I just think it's too early and we still working on us."

"Yeah, I guess you right."

"Plus, my family different from others really."

"They racist or something?" Lil Smoke knew how Spanish families in Miami were. They wanted their daughters and females in the family to stick to their own kind.

"No, not at all. They just have different understanding."

"I got it."

"When the time is right, it will come lead focus on this, papi." She reached over the table, almost spilling his drink to give him a kiss.

The two enjoyed the rest of their date with a walk on a beach. Something neither one of them did before, so the night was a big vibe.

Walking hand to hand on the beach set off the right energy for both. Someone was in the water sending fireworks into the sky, giving off the fourth July atmosphere.

Chapter 28
West Miami

KVon woke up to a new woman that he met a few weeks ago. Shit had been going real good between them, so he was feeling her energy.

Today, he had a lot of shit to take care of. He tapped Trinny, looking at her fat ass poke out of the covers.

"Wake up, shawty," KVon said.

"Morning daddy," Trinny said, rubbing her hand between his legs, trying to get that morning wake up.

"Not right now, I got things to do, okay," KVon told her, putting on his slippers.

"You want me to cook for you?" She asked mainly for herself because her stomach was flipping.

"Sure, just don't burn down my kitchen. I'ma take a shower." KVon went into his walk-in closet that led to the private bathroom. KVon loved living a lush lifestyle; everything had to be top of the line.

Walking into the bathroom, he saw a fake Gucci purse. He could tell it was a knock off by the logo. KVon knew it had to be Trinny's. He picked it up to feel a vibration. Something in his head told him to look in the back but another side told KVon to give it to Trinny.

After a few seconds of thinking, he opened the bag and saw a pill bottle and an iPhone with a message across her screen reading, *"Is he dead yet?"*

The look on KVon's face said it all, as he looked at the pill bottle to see a hazard sign. KVon couldn't pronounce the name on the bottle but he could tell it was poison. He easily put two and two together.

KVon smelled eggs and sausages cooking in the kitchen so he quickly came up with a little plan, leaving the purse where he found it.

"Baby," KVon yelled.

"Yes, daddy, I thought you was getting in the shower," Trinny said, turning around in nothing but a thong and a bra, showing her big plastic ass.

"I'm starving so I'ma take a shower after." KVon sat down and watched her cook the meal with a big smile upon his face.

"You good, baby. The food is done."

"Okay, let's eat."

"I made a special meal for you. Trust me, you will love it." Trinny brought him over a plate and herself a sandwich with some orange juice.

"Hmm, looks good," KVon said about to dig in as she stared. Then, he paused and looked up.

"What's wrong?" She asked, hoping he ate.

"Have a bite."

"Oh, no thank you. This sandwich is more than enough." She quickly took a bite of her sandwich.

"I'm not asking you, Trinny. I'm telling you right now!" KVon got serious.

"What's gotten into you. I'm full, baby." She got nervous, seeing him get up.

"You right, my love. I just wanted you to eat healthy," KVon said, softly rubbing her shoulders.

"I'm okay, baby but you need to eat," she replied, enjoying the massage.

"Never bitch! Who sent you?" KVon yelled as he started choking the life out of her, cutting off her oxygen.

"The cop," she spoke when she could.

"Who bitch? What cop?"

"He offered me money to poison you. I don't know his name," Trinny cried before KVon broke her neck, already knowing who it was now.

***

Neither one of them knew how they ended up in the bed together at Lil Trap's new crib next door to Lil Smoke. Solan came over to chill and order pizza, then shit got heated real quick.

"I hope you eat this pussy to the T." Solan moaned before sitting on his face, letting her freaky side come out.

Lil Trap wasted no time as he swirled his tongue over her wet clit, teasing her as Solan started to ride his face.

"Uhmm, fuck!" She screamed while he sucked her clit until she came all over his face. Solan yearned for some dick. She hopped off his face and, on the bed, laying on her back.

"You like it," Lil Trap said, sliding effortlessly into her drenched pussy. Solan screamed, feeling him deep inside her walls.

Lil Trap saw she was trying to pull his dick out, but he moved her little hands. He spread her legs open like a V while wrapping his hands around her throat. Solan soon came hard on her first real double orgasm.

"Oh my God. Fuck me doggie style," she eagerly begged.

"Solan's body laid convulsing under him as he flipped her over, watching her arch her back and give him a visual. Solan felt him enter and threw her ass back on the pole as she made it jiggle and clap on his lower stomach.

"Damn shawty, do that shit," Lil Trap gritted out, trying to hold his nut. The pussy was so fire.

"I'm cumming, daddy. Choke me!" She yelled out as Lil Trap went one step extra. He slid a thumb in her ass and grabbed her throat with his free hand.

"Fuckkkk!" She cried, cumming all over his cock as Lil Trap legs started to shake. He busted his nut, but Solan quickly pulled him out and raced for his dick with her lips.

Solan sucked him until all the warm, thick cum was down her throat like a true soldier.

"What the hell?" Lil Trap watched her make love to his penis.

"I told you I could get freaky." She giggled, wiping the cum string hanging from her chin.

"Let's take a shower."

"Can we fuck in there?" Solan asked a dumb question because that was his plan anyway.

Romell Tukes

Chapter 29
Miami Dade, Miami

Sacqo loved waking up in his four-million-dollar home that he got off drug money. It had been years of him dealing with his connect and very close friend Royal. The two met years ago in LA on a business trip for a weed connect. Sacqo was selling bud in Kentucky at the time before he flooded the state with coke and dope.

Once they formed a trust bond, then came the business bond, which led to them both being able to get rich off each other. Every summer, he would come spend time at his Miami mansion plus he could be close to Royal. Normally, he was in Kentucky surrounded by Mexicans.

He turned around to see his young girl, Evenly, a beautiful Cuban woman he only dealt with when coming to Miami. Evenly wasn't in sight, so he figured she took the 10,000 he gave her to go shopping today.

Sacqo had a maid and a personal chef who made food every morning but today he didn't smell a thing. He made his way downstairs starving but, on his way, down, he saw something that startled him.

There was a group of men standing in his living room over two dead bodies. One was his maid and the other he recognized as the house chef. The crazy part of it all was looking at Evenly hang from the ceiling fan on a rope with blood pouring down her pretty face as if someone punched on her for weeks. A chair was the only thing saving her life at the moment.

"Sacqo, nice of you to visit Miami again. I've been waiting on your arrival," the unfamiliar man said, standing up from the chair that he had been sitting in for close to an hour.

"Who are you?" The fear in Sacqo's voice could be heard miles away.

"My name is Mucho."

When Sacqo heard the name, his eyes widened, and heart pounded with fear from hearing the name while dealing. "I didn't do nothing to bring this disrespect to my home."

"That's where you wrong. Anybody who fuck with my opps are my opps also. Sacqo, wrong team," Mucho said, pulling out a gun. He proceeded to fire six shots in Evenly's body, killing her then kicking the chair from under her feet.

"Nooo, not her." Sacqo had many tears as some of Mucho guards tried to control their laughs. An hour ago, Evenly was trying to give them Sacqo's safe number, family member info, bank account, and social security number just to save her own ass.

"What do you want, please?"

"Royal." Mucho kept it short and easy.

"Today, at 1pm, we have a meeting," Sacqo said, crying.

"Where?"

"North Miami. Man, you killed the love of my life." Sacqo looked up at Evenly's gruesomely murdered body, crying to his higher power.

"You're going to join her now. I'll do you that favor."

"Oh no, I'll get over it." Sacqo quickly got himself together, not wanting to die with seven kids to raise.

"Sometimes we don't always get what we want in life."

Boc ... Boc ... Boc ... Boc ... Boc ...

Mucho and his crew exit the crib. He said he had to kill the chef because he gave Mucho the drop on Sacqo.

***

University of Miami, Miami

Alina recently changed her major to Forensic which basically is the trained professed pf exa,omomg the autolysis, decomposition in human, and studying the crime scene that a person was murdered at. Her professor preached in front of the class while all fifty students took perfect notes, including Alina.

"We all know autolysis means self-digestion that occurs immediately after a person has died. When the carbon dioxide in a body builds up, it becomes acidic. This is what the surface of the skin looks like when the internal organs develop blisters," Professor Landy said, clicking on pictures of dead bodies on his projector board.

"The blisters are filled with nutrients and soon, the top layer of skin will loosen away from the underlying structure." Alina said, out in front of the class.

"Nice Alina, so can you tell me the next stage when a body is decomposed?" The professor asked.

"The bloating phase is the bacteria that's already present which changes the color of a person's skin. The body could then grow to twice its normal size. I believe the next stage will be the body mass loss leaving the bones, hair, and cartilage known as the decay stage. I believe." Alina been doing some studying and for a person to just have started the class at the beginning of a new semester, they were all shocked. The students and her professor.

"Wow, very well, Alina."

"Thanks," she replied.

"Question, since you know the stages very well, can you tell me the timeline that demonstrates the time and death which can be estimated based on the state of the human remains?" Professor Landy confused his whole class with this question because he never went over the timeline period.

"Okay, I think it's 24-72 hours after death, dealing with decomposition of internal organs. Three to five days after death, the bloating appears and foam leaks from the victim's nose and mouth. Eight to ten days after death, the color changes. A month later, liquefaction of the body occurs," Alina said, hearing claps from students who didn't know if she was right or wrong, but it sounded legit.

"I must say I'm impressed. Maybe you should teach next class?" The professor asked

"No way, I'm good." Alina response made the class laugh as they went on with their next lesson for the day. Alina's mind switched over to Lil Smoke as she wondered what he was doing so Alina texted him.

***

Overtown, Miami

Lil Smoke overslept. He was out all night, scoping a trap house in Lil Haiti that the nigga KVon was running. The trap was making a lot of money and Lil Smoke wanted a piece of it without having to turn into the Hulk. Being a businessman, Lil Smoke knew it's not all about violence or bloodshed. Sometimes, a simple talk can do the job. Nafee went out to a nearby mosque with Emma who been in the crib more than him. Lil Smoke didn't really care for Emma, but he thought she was perfect for Nafee. Now that Lil Trap moved across the hall, he knew there was nowhere to run. Looking at his iPhone, a text from Alina popped up asking what he was doing. Lil Smoke hit back, telling her he was about to take a shower and chill.

***

North Miami, Miami

Royal loved gold for years now. It became a guilty pleasure, then a hobby that he had to do three to five times a month. Over the years, Royal met a lot of wealthy people that he ended up doing business with later down the line.

Two security guards posted on the golf cart, trying to avoid the hot sun as Royal golfed like he was a pro.

"I can show you fuck faces how to golf instead of riding bulls and fighting fucking chickens all day." Royal guards were all mostly from home back in Mexico. Every week, he recruited twenty or more.

"We don't golf, boss," one of the guards stated.

"That's because you can't afford to. Now, call Sacqo and see where he's at." Royal checked his watch, seeing his client was a few minutes late.

"No answer, Royal."

"What?" Royal stopped his swing in mid stroke, walking to the golf cart pissed off. He hated lateness. It was disrespectful. That was something his uncle always taught him.

Royal called but no answer. He had other shit to do so he gathered everything and got on the back of the golf cart, riding to the front.

The golf club was so big a person could easily get lost but Royal made it to the front quickly but something inside of him told Royal to look near the restroom area when they parked. Royal looked at a small army with guns and Mucho led the pack. When they locked eyes, it was on and popping.

Tat, Tat, Tat, Tat, Tat, Tat, Tat, Tat …

Bloc, Bloc, Bloc, Bloc, Bloc …

Mucho goons knocked off both of Royal men as they moved too slowly to react unlike Royal, who was racing for the parking lot, He was firing back every chance he got. Bullets were hot on Royal's ass, but he managed to get in his car that was hailed down with live rounds from all types of assault rifles. Mucho saw the Bentley race out the lot and became furious because he had his rival in a corner, but he got away with ease.

Romell Tukes

Chapter 30
Miami, FL
One week later

Lil Smoke got a call from Lura early this morning telling him to take an Uber to the airport and go to the private landing strip area.

One thing he came to realize with Lura was never question, just follow her lead. The product was almost done anyway. Give or take, he had three to six kilos left in the cut. Having niggas like Bowy on the squad was the reason shit been moving so fast and perfect.

The only thing in his way was KVon. The guy was becoming a big problem and Lil Smoke knew he needed to put an end to him very soon. Jiam also been laying low, but Lil Smoke came up with a little plan for him.

Arriving at the airport, he went through TSA security and made his way to the jet he saw Lura waiting in front of, dressed in a Chanel business suit.

"Hey," Lil Smoke said looking at the large jet.

"You ready?" She said walking up the stairs of the jet.

Lil Smoke followed Lura, looking at her nicely shaped ass and smelling her Chanel perfume, wondering if she had a man because Lura seemed to focus on strictly business.

"Ever been on a private jet, youngster?" Lura asked, getting comfortable taking off her high heels.

"No." Lil Smoke looked around to see butter leather seats, flat screen TVs, laptops, small bars, and a bedroom connected to a bathroom.

"Get relaxed. We going to PR."

"Where your guards at?" asked Lil Smoke.

"They home. You my personal guard for the day, my love." Lura pushed a button on the wall and a small compartment flipped open with two handguns. She passed one to Lil Smoke and placed one in her purse for safety measures.

"Okay. I'm down for that." Lil Smoke tucked the weapon, seeing her smile at him.

"I see you upped your style in dressing." She peeped his Louis Vuitton denim set and sneakers to match.

"Learned from the best."

"How's the product moving for your crew? Any slips?"

"The money is good, and product been moving at a fast rate. I'm ready for a new shipment. I been meaning to call you."

"Wow, I'm proud of you. Take your time. No need to rush. Me and Mucho will always be here," she shot back.

"I already know. I just like to stay consistent." Lil Smoke stared out the window while Lura took a nap. She looked so sexy sleep. He had to stop staring. He was starting to feel like a creep.

***

San Juan, PR

Lura and Lil Smoke exit the jet, climbing in a black Jeep Wrangler truck sent by Angia, the queenpin. She was who they came to see and make business arrangements with.

"Don't let this bitch's looks fuck up your train of thought." Lura said, making their way through the capital.

"Got you." Lil Smoke had no clue why he was here, but he'd just roll with the punches.

The mansion was big, but it was in old style fashion because the place got built in the 18th century.

Entering the front, big doors, a tall older man spoke a few words into the walkie talkie. Then, let both of his boss guests to the living room area, which was on the other side of the house.

"This shit is fly," Lil Smoke said, walking through the hallways.

"I've saw better," Lura added as the guard walked into the all-white and gray living room.

Lil Smoke saw one of the biggest asses he ever saw in person. When Angia turned around, she had to be straight out of a modeling magazine. Lura saw the look on Lil Smoke's face as if he couldn't stop staring at Angia's ass and body in them tight leggings.

"Lura, it's so nice to see you again," Angina said, giving Lura a friendly hug.

"Same to you, Angia. You still beautiful I see," Lura lied.

"Not as sexy as you." Angia flirted back, meaning every word. She was looking Lura up and down, thinking nasty as her bisexual side kicked in.

"Like what you've done to the place." Lura looked around.

"Thanks, but who is this?" Angia asked, looking at Lil Smoke.

"Sorry, how rude. This is Lil Smoke, one of my most trusted workers," Lura bragged.

"Oh, so young but very handsome. Come have a sit." Angina smiled at Lil Smoke, peaking at his dick print.

Angia was the biggest coke supplier in PR. It was passed down to her from her mother who died five years ago due to a stroke.

"I wanted to speak with you about me and Mucho supplying you," said Lura.

"No, I'm good," Angia replied quickly as if she knew her reason of coming.

"Look, this is business. I heard your supply went dry a few months back. I honestly just want to help," Lura stated, seeing Angia and her guard laugh.

"Lura, if I needed help, I would've found it. Trust me. I'm doing very fine out here. I'm still the queen of Puerto Rico my love," Angina bragged, feeling like the boss bitch she truly was.

"I understand. Do you have a ladies' room that I can use before I leave?" Lura asked.

"Yes, down the hall to your left, mami. No hard feelings. You know how business is." Angia smirked.

"Yes, I do." Lura respectfully stood to use the ladies' room, leaving.

"Lil Smoke, where you from handsome?" Angina got closer to him.

"Miami." Lil Smoke got uncomfortable.

"I can tell but how about I take you to another level in the game and make you richer than you could dream of?" She told him, touching his hair.

"I'm straight with Lura. She's family but thank you anyway," he shot back, seeing her smile turn upside down.

"When her and Mucho cross you after using you, my door will be open handsome," Angina said moving back into her original spot, wondering why Lura was taking so long.

Lil Smoke couldn't help but think what Angia meant when she said they will cross him, but he also knew the mind games people played.

"Let's start over!" Lura yelled out, getting everybody's attention as she had Angia's fourteen year old son in front of her with a gun to his head.

Angia's security guard reached for his pistol, but Lil smoke popped him twice in the neck and once in his heart, finishing the tall man.

"Lura, please, I'll do whatever." Angia got on her knees, begging. She loved her son.

"Bitch, there is nothing you can do. This whole time you been working for Royal," Lura stated.

"Yes, but it's only business. I need a plug."

"Looks like you chose the wrong connect," Lura said, before putting a bullet in the kid's head and then killing Angia.

Lil Smoke couldn't believe his eyes. Lura was a real savage. He followed her out the mansion as they killed two armed men outside, taking the jeep back to the jet to go home.

Chapter 31
North, Miami

Lil Smoke wanted to get out the house tonight, so he called Alina, but she was busy studying for an exam at the end of the week. She promised tomorrow night they could spend the night together because she missed him also.

Lil Trap called him right on time as him and Bowy was already in a club having a good time, drinking and vibing.

The trip to PR went odd but Lil Smoke didn't know what to expect from the jump, so he wasn't even mad . But now, there was no question to how crazy Lura really could get.

There wasn't a line outside so Lil Smoke walked in the packed club, nodding to the Pooh Sheisty music while making his way through the large crowd. Looking up toward the second level, he saw Bowy and Lil Trap getting bottles in ice buckets with sparkles as if it was someone's birthday.

"Lil Smoke!" a dark chick yelled out from behind.

"Tish, what's up, shawty?" Lil Smoke remembered her from school.

"I haven't seen you in forever," she told him with a slur in her voice from drinking all day.

"How's everything?"

"I'm fine, working and shit. I came out to have a good time before somebody get the shooting in this bitch." She looked around, knowing how drunk Miami niggas get.

"Come up to the VIP. Lil Trap up there."

"Oh, I heard he was locked up on a murder," she said following him upstairs.

"Nope, he good," Lil Smoke spoke, walking into the VIP section to the smell of weed.

"Tish, what the fuck," Lil Trap stated seeing how thick she was now. He used to have a crush on Tish in school but never told her.

"You look different," Tish said, giving him a hug before sitting on the club couch.

"Bowy, I see you doing your thing, bruh." Lil Smoke looked at Bowy and the cute redbone in his arms.

"She a winner, bruh," Bowy replied back, gassing the young lady up.

"You still fucking with Fats?" Lil Trap asked, knowing Fats was her boo thang.

"On and off. He be fucking with them Pork N Beans too much," she said sounding disgusted.

"I thought he was out of Liberty City?" Lil Smoke asked.

"He is but dude fucking with Jiam and them crazy niggas," Tish said, not even seeing the look on everybody's face in the VIP section.

"Damn, that's crazy. You look like you could use a drink," Lil Smoke suggested, handing her a cold bottle of Patron out of the ice bucket.

"Thank you," Tish shot back before drinking and talking all night long, giving up Fats new location more than once.

When the club was close to shutting down, Tish was knocked out, snoring on the couch right where the gang left her ass. They were planning to pay Fats a visit.

***

South, Miami

Bowy wanted to take his new joint out to get a bite to eat before going to a hotel for the nightcap.

"What's your name again?" Bowy asked, turning down the Lil Baby and Lil Durk album he'd been rocking to for a whole week now.

"You serious?" She stopped rubbing his inner thighs and got mad.

"I know your name, on everything, I was just capping." Bowy turned the music back on trying to play it off.

"What's my name, Bowy?" She turned the music down furious.

"It starts with a B, shawty. Calm down." Bowy pulled into the Waffle House parking lot.

"Nigga, it's Shasay. You got me fucked up. What I look like!" She shouted, making a scene as he parked the Benz, trying his hardest not to laugh.

"Babe, I was fucking with you. Come on, how could I not know your name." He grabbed her fat pussy under her skirt.

"Uhmmmm, you better." She bit her lips, feeling the wetness leak down her thick thighs.

"Let's eat then. I'ma take care of this water leak after." He saw his finger was dripping with her juices.

"Okay, I'm starving anyway. I had a good time with your friends," she stated, getting out of the car, and walking by his side in the 24 hour Waffle House everybody came to after clubbing.

"Yeah, Lil Smoke and Lil Trap are family. We about to take over the city, shawty," Bowy said, making sure his pistol was tucked so it wouldn't fall.

"Lil Trap, I think I've heard of him."

"Maybe, but what you ordering?" He asked, sitting down, looking around to see a bunch of nobody's with their crew or girls just chilling.

"Order me whatever. I got to go to the lady room." Shasay took her purse with her.

"Hurry up back." Bowy watched her fat ass bounced all over the place as he thought about all the sexual moves, he planned to do with her soon.

An hour later, they both were ready to leave and hit the hotel to fuck. Walking in the parking lot, a black truck pulled up and Shasay turned, trying to rush back in the restaurant but Bowy grabbed her wrist.

Two gunmen hopped out the truck with choppers, spraying rounds inside the Waffle House and at Bowy, who used Shasay as a shield until he got to his car. He tossed her on the ground.

Bloc, Bloc, Bloc, Bloc … Tat, Tat, Tat, Tat, Tat, Tat …

Bowy hit one of the gunmen but two more exited the other side. When Bowy saw this, he got in the Benz, peeling off. He hit two parked cars, but he made it out safely.

Shasay was Jiam's niece. When she went to use the restroom, she told Jiam that she was with Lil Trap's people. Shasay knew about the beef because she was nosy and deep in the streets, selling clothes and pussy for a dollar.

Chapter 32
Liberty City, Miami

Fats smoked a blunt of fire weed with his boy Tic, watching the TV that he had install of the Cadillac dashboard. The car was pimped out on twenty-eight inch rims, sky blue and white paint job, loud system, and custom seats.

Since getting money with Jiam, his life changed. He became an overnight success story in his hood, Liberty City. He sold weight to a few niggas he knew for years but the young niggas around his way been taking over, just like in Carol City.

Everywhere he looked, young niggas was locking shit down and he had been meaning to tell Jiam about it. Fats had been too busy with court, child support, and chasing pussy.

"This my show, bruh. On my mama," Tic said, watching Family Guy, taking deep pulls and almost coughing up a lung.

"Damn, bruh. Pass my shit, folk." Fats reached for the blunt and that's when he saw a gun pointed in the window.

"Oh shit."

Bloc ... Bloc ... Bloc ... Bloc...

Bullets ripped through Tic's skull, killing him as Fats quickly reached for his door. He climbed out with his ass hanging out. When he turned to run, Lil Smoke's gun smashed into his forehead, taking him clean out.

Lil Trap and Lil Smoke tossed Fats in the Scooby Doo van as Nafee pulled away from the crime scene, headed to a remote location in some woods.

Twenty minutes later, the van drove up a trail outside of Coconut Grove behind a lake area. People came out to fish in the daytime but at night, it turned into mystery lake.

"This nigga still sleep cuz," Lil Trap said, slapping Fats until he woke up to see he had real cuffs on his wrist and feet.

"Mama, help," mumbled Fats as Nafee tried his best not to laugh.

"This is it right here," Lil Smoke said seeing the two blue containers he placed there earlier for an easy way to dismember bodies and scatter other remains of a human body.

"Let's drag his fat ass out." Lil Trap opened the doors and dragged Fats, who was crying and screaming.

"Nobody can hear you, big boy," Lil Smoke told him, pulling out a saw and ax.

"Who are you?" Fats yelled, getting a good look at the men. He saw it was Lil Trap and Lil Smoke.

"Nigga don't play. Tell me what you know about Jiam," Lil Smoke spoke, standing in the light.

Fats saw who it was and laughed at them because he thought real killers had him. "Man, y'all bitch ass niggas get me out these cuffs," Fats said, not taking them serious.

"One more time, Fats. I need info on Jiam and KVon." Lil Smoke was patient.

"Fuck y'all niggas! I'ma kill both of you." Fats blurted out before Lil Smoke's ax swung at his head, taking it clean off.

"What the fuck?" Lil Trap just witnessed a man's head come clean off.

"Put the head in the small oil drum and I'ma burn the remains in this big container," Lil Smoke said, not fazed one bit by his actions.

"Y'all niggas be doing the most," Nafee said from the driver seat, not trying to watch the scene because he had a weak stomach.

"Help us," Lil Smoke coached.

"Fuck nah, nigga." Nafee turned back around, minding his own business as Lil Smoke placed Fats' body in the container, lighting it on fire watching it burn but leaving the head to remain.

***

Khadija watched the gruesome scene from a distance with night vision goggles that she loved to use on night missions.

Trying to keep up with Lil Smoke had been a little hard but she finally caught up with him today and swore to keep tabs on the crew.

Seeing Lil Smoke kill the man using an axe, she may have underestimated his ability to kill.

Every time she used an axe to kill someone, it would normally take four to five swings just to take off a clean head.

Watching the youngins burn the body, she was a little impressed but that wouldn't save Lil Smoke from the grips of her death she had for him one bit.

Now seeing Lil Smoke's two man crew, she came to a thought of killing them all because they could turn out to be a problem eventually. Not hearing from Emma made her a little nervous because she was nowhere to be found and she got rid of the old phone number she used to have.

Umer called Khadija two nights ago talking about some dumb shit. He still thought Khadija set him up in Brooklyn where he almost lost his life. After trying to accuse her, Umer then claimed his brother could of most likely been the one who tried to take him out. That's when she hung up the phone call.

Khadija made it clear to Umer that if she wanted him dead, it would've happened a long time ago and it would've involved a lot of pain.

The van pulled out of the dark wooded area, speeding on to the highway. She tried to keep up and still play a distance, so she'll be unnoticed.

Five minutes later, the van parked in some large complex surrounded by cars and fences Khadija parked on the outside, wondering what the fuck they were doing now. The lot was pitch black and with all the cars in her way, Khadija could barely see.

Seconds later, three cars came flying out the lot going different ways, leaving her in a confusing position.

"Little fuckers," she shouted, losing them all this time.

Khadija had to admit. The crew was very smart and covered their tracks. She had a new respect for them after the move they just did. She figured they had a feeling someone was on them. She thought it would be good to give Lil Smoke space and focus back on her life.

Romell Tukes

Chapter 33
Miami Dade County, Miami

Mucho had a big dinner prepared for today, something he used to normally do before his life got super busy. He was dealing with Lura, Mexico, his girlfriend, and the Royal situation.

Missing his target a few weeks ago made Mucho feel like he was losing it. Back in the day, Mucho used to be a great shooter but now, as he is getting older, he sees that decreasing.

Walking downstairs, he could smell the good Mexican food in the air as he slowly inhaled.

"Lura!" He yelled, seeing if she was back from her exercise because they had to go over a few things before his trip back to Mexico.

"What, nigga?" She yelled, sticking he head out of her room door where she was getting dressed.

"I'm not your nigga and hurry up. Since, when you started taking hours to get ready for dinner?" he yelled walking off.

"Give me a few!" She shouted back, slamming her door, and mumbling to herself.

"Stupid," Mucho said, walking back into the kitchen to see the maids and head chef in the kitchen doing their thing. They were cooking up all types of Spanish food.

"Smelling good, how long?" Mucho asked, smelling inside of a pot.

"Twenty minutes, boss," a white man replied, who was the cook, flipping baked fish inside the steel and cement oven.

"Perfect." Mucho walked out the kitchen to hear the doorbell ring.

"Get the door. That's Lil Smoke," Lura yelled from upstairs.

"Lil Smoke was coming." Mucho had no clue the boy was even invited to tonight's dinner, but he didn't mind.

"Big Smoke," Mucho joked.

"Mucho, good to see you. Thanks for inviting me," Lil Smoke said, walking inside.

"Of course, youngin. You are family. Plus, I needed to see you anyway. I've been so busy out of town and making moves."

"I understand, Mucho. No need to explain."

"Okay, how the drugs moving out there?"

"Shit been going fast. It's really pure and uncut so the people are loving it a lot." Lil Smoke got a lot of good feedback on the product he had been getting.

"Okay, that's what I like to hear, kid. The financial reports been raising, so I would really like to applaud you for your hard work," Mucho stated sincerely.

"Business is business," he shot back, seeing Lura come downstairs in a sexy, gold dress, hugging her curves. Mucho had not saw Lura dress like this in a long time. He looked more shocked than Lil Smoke.

"Hey," Lura said to Lil Smoke, who was silent at a loss of words.

"You going out?" Mucho asked.

"Maybe, but when is the next order?" She asked.

"In a few days, I'm sure of." Mucho confirmed as the food was delivered to the dinner table.

"I have to send twenty percent to Texas and Las Vegas."

"Got you, but have you heard about Angia?" Mucho asked, not knowing she worked for Royal. Lura shook her head, sadly acting if she didn't know. Lil Smoke played dumb thinking how cold Lura was.

***

Carol City, Miami
Two days later

Lil Smoke looked at the number of kilos on the living room floor and divided it into three sections as Nafee did the math on his laptop. Nafee added up each brick's street value and how much they were supposed to receive back in profits.

"I'ma fill the bando tonight," Bowy said, thinking about his trap house he had around the corner.

The whole living room was covered in a stack of keys. It looked like some movie type shit off Scarface.

"You did the math for each section except mine because I'ma place it in the stash for a rainy day. I meant to do that before, but I forgot we had a lot going on," said Lil Smoke.

"We still do, bro. These niggas starting to get on my last nerves," Lil Trap protested ready to turn it up a notch.

"Chill out, Jim Jones. The serial killer shit take time. We not dealing with low life street dealers," Nafee added as Lil Trap looked at Nafee, rolling his eyes.

"Nigga, you not even in the field, cuz. You a driver and our financial aid advisor," Lil Trap yelled, making Bowy laugh as Lil Smoke walked off. He already knew where this shit was going.

"Look, bruh. Anybody can be a killer, but that shit don't mean shit to me, bruh. I can fight. I don't need a gun." Nafee gave Lil Trap a look as if he was challenging his manhood.

"What you saying, cuz?" Lil Trap got hype real quick, feeling played.

"Take it how you want to take it, bitch nigga." Nafee spat as the room got silent and Bowy got out of the way.

Lil Trap punched Nafee in the face with a clean shot but didn't expect for Nafee to tackle him, putting Lil Trap on his back and punching him in the face.

They wrestled, punched, kicked, and bit each other for five minutes until they got tired. Both had black eyes and busted lips. Bowy and Lil Smoke watched the whole shit, laughing at how goofy they looked. It was coming sooner or later because the two of them been going at each other since Fats' death. Lil Trap disliked the fact Nafee never put in work like he did.

"Y'all fools done?" Lil Smoke asked.

"Nah, I want another round," Nafee said, feeling his busted lip

"Let's get it, hoe nigga." Lil Trap attacked Nafee, falling top of the bricks, swinging and

missing Nafee. Nafee hopped back on his feet, catching Lil Trap with a two piece.

"Damn," Bowy laughed, seeing Lil Trap lose his balance from the impact but got himself back.

Lil Trap caught Nafee with an uppercut, making him spit out blood. They started wrestling like pro wrestlers but were really tired.

When they had no more gas, both men needed water as blood was all over Bowy's stash house. He barely came to it since he got it two weeks ago.

"Who paying for my rugs? I'm not fighting. I'ma shoot one of you niggas." Bowy walked to the back, pissed off as Nafee and Lil Trap ice grilled each other before going different ways. They left Lil Smoke with the product.

Chapter 34
Lil Haiti, Miami

Slip loved Saturday nights because the trap house would rake in at least 30 to 40,000 dollars in one day of working out the bando. All the crackheads came through the backdoor to cop dimes, dubs, or grams. It was a crazy setup.

He had been working for KVon since he was fourteen years old. Slip recently turned twenty.

"Slip, can I take off tonight? I ain't got no babysitter for Sammy," says a chubby bitch named Meka, who worked Slip as a dealer. Meka's job was to collect the money from the fiends whenever they arrived. Jordan would hand over the product while Slip's shooter, Big Head posted up with a Draco.

"Bitch, you not going nowhere," Slip told her, about to get upset.

"Slip, come on. She needs to go, and I can cover for her," Jordan says, rubbing his arm.

Jordan was a bad, slim redbone with long red dreads that went down to the crack of her ass.

"Bitch, did I ask you?" Slip slapped the shit out of Jordan as Big Head laughed on his stool in the kitchen.

"Damn, Slip. Is it like that? After I suck you off all day," Jordan cried.

"It's too late to leave, shawty. Them people 'bout to slide through. We finna open up shop. Unlock that backdoor, Big Head. Let's get this paper, folk." Slip nodded at his longtime friend.

"Gotcha cuz." Big Head unlocked the backdoor as the ladies passed each other a G pack of crack, which was a thousand dollars' worth of hard cooked crack ready to be sold.

"Look at this nigga. First one." Slip joked at the man rocking a hoodie that it was too hot for outside, but nobody paid it no mind. Jordan.

"It's too hot for that shit," Jordan said when the man stepped foot on the porch. He smoothly went behind his back.

The hooded man pulled out a gun and blew Big Head's brains on the kitchen wall. He kicked the body to the floor as two more men entered.

Slip didn't know what to do when he saw all the guns aimed at him and the girls.

"You had a good run, cuz but shit over now," Lil Trap stated, pulling off his mask and pointing the 357 handgun he carried.

"The drugs all on the table and the money is in the top cabinet. It's all yours, bruh." Slip placed his hands in the air, surrendering.

"Nigga, shut the fuck up. Where can we find your cousin?" Bowy asked, seeing one of the women give him a strange stare.

"KVon don't be out. I barely see bruh. Jiam's people drop me off my work now." Slip prayed to God that he made it out of this. If so, he was going to church on Sunday with his mom.

"I got a feeling you lying." Bowy moved closer to Slip. Then, it hit him. The redbone in the spot was his first girlfriend.

"Jordan?" Bowy couldn't believe it. he thought she moved back to Texas in the fifth grade.

"Bowy, that's you?" Jordan asked, still shaking in fear.

"Where you been at?"

"My mom sent me back to Texas, but she sent me back to Miami. I missed you," says Jordan as everybody around the room looked at each other.

"What the fuck is this? Love Connection?" Lil Trap burst out, shooting Slip and the two women, killing them all.

Bowy wanted to punch Lil Trap in the face, but his face was already swollen from the Nafee fight.

"That was all for what?" Bowy looked at Jordan's dead body and felt some type of way.

"Let's go. Niggas made the spot hot for nothing." Lil Smoke looked at Lil Trap, who didn't give a fuck.

"I look pussy?" Bowy got in Lil Trap's face, ready to fight.

"You trying make love to a bitch in a crack house while we trying to get info. Bruh, get real, cuz."

"Aight, folk." Bowy rushed out, throwing on his hoodie and brushing pass both men.

"You could have let them talk." Lil Smoke ain't know what gotten into Trap but he been on a different type of time.

"Fuck her, bro," Lil Trap replied, walking out of the spot with no remorse.

***

Downtown, Miami

Dr. Akbar arrived at a fancy seafood restaurant to meet up with Lil Smoke to check on him. Today would've been his wife's birthday. All day, memories of them flooded his head. Earlier, his beautiful daughter called him to check on her father because she knew what today was.

Checking his watch, Lil Smoke walked in with a cool bop, looking around before the doctor waived him down.

"Dr. Akbar, nice to see you." Lil Smoke extended his hand out to give him a firm manly handshake.

"Likewise, young brother. I see you looking like Savage more and more every day. I swear by Allah."

"I want to thank you again for everything, doc." Lil Smoke skipped over his comment about his brother. Anytime someone spoke about Savage, he would get uncomfortable and try to avoid it because the subject was touchy.

"No problem, kiddo. You are family, and I will always try to help whenever possible."

"How's your daughter?"

"Great, working hard. She is a workaholic." Dr Akbar joked but dead serious. His baby girl worked nonstop and focused on school.

Lil Smoke didn't want to admit it, but he had a little crush on his daughter. Even Dr. Akbar could tell, and he didn't mind because Lil Smoke was a good kid deep down. He just chose the wrong lifestyle.

"You like her, don't you?"

"Huh, me. Oh, no," Lil Smoke lied

"It's okay because she also inquired about you a few days ago." Dr. Akbar saw him almost fall out of his seat.

"Really, what did she say?" He looked so surprised.

"Got you," Dr. Akbar laughed.

"She likes your character. We all do but there is more for you out here than the streets, son," Dr. Akbar said as they enjoyed the lunch meeting.

Chapter 35
Overtown, Miami

Nafee had been counting money all day for the clique because money machines wasn't his thing. He preferred the old school way. The gang had been stacking so much money lately. He concluded that they would need another stash house.

While driving back home, he thought about the fight he had with Lil Trap's wild ass.

He e saw the fight coming for days before. Dealing with niggas like Lil Trap, he knew the only way to earn their respect is by fucking them up.

Being a gangster was never in Nafee's plans. He liked college and training himself for success, not being in the streets. He felt like Lil Smoke needed him while in the street to cover his back.

His cell phone rang, and it was his dad, Yasir calling. He picked up while stopped at a red light.

"Assalamualaikum," Nafee answered.

"Wa alaikum salaam," Yasir replied, sounding like he was driving.

"I ain't heard from you in a few weeks, pops." Nafee thought a van was following him.

"I've been working hard, son and trying to open a new plumbing location in Broward County with Hira. You know she's the business minded one." Yasir laughed but speaking the truth because Hira was very smart.

"That's good, pops. I miss y'all."

"I know you do. Y'all should've never moved," his father stated.

"I had to start my adulthood some way and us moving out had to be a start." Nafee didn't want to tell his dad how he became a killer and drug dealer overnight. Even though, Yasir shared stories with him 'bout his years in the dangerous lifestyle.

"Understood, how's your brother?" Yasir referred to Lil Smoke as his brother since they were kids.

"Going crazy over a girlfriend now." Yasir laughed because Lil Smoke used to talk about how much he hated women growing up. Yasir was just glad he wasn't gay.

"Yeah, I got one too. Her name is Emma. She African and Muslim."

"Muslim, wow. Humduliallah, young brother. You deserve a woman that Allah provides. Stay on your deen and marry her."

"I plan to. I really think she is the one."

"That's good to hear, son. When will I see her and all of you again?" Yasir asked.

"Soon. I just been a little busy"

"What's soon? Don't spin me around, boy. I can tell when you lying to me because you fumble over your words."

"I'ma come to Jummah, Friday," Nafee promised.

"Bring your brother, too."

"I'll try dad. You know how he is."

"I don't care. Bring him! I love y'all." Yasir hung up the phone right when Nafee pulled up to the crib.

Inside, Emma was cleaning up, wearing cute booty shorts with ass hanging out. She was fresh off her period. Nafee ain't waste no time. He locked the door, grabbed her from behind and started to kiss her neck. Seconds later, Nafee was fucking the shit out of Emma all over the kitchen floor as she screamed in pleasure. Then, they took it to the showers.

***

Hours later

Alina collapsed on the bed after riding Lil Smoke's dick in a reverse cowgirl position. She going so crazy that she almost snapped his manhood in half.

"Baby, you must have really missed me." Lil Smoke joked laying there, thinking about how good Alina's pussy be when he fucking her.

"Shut up." She playfully punched him in his chest.

"What time you got to be back at school," he asked, making sure she was on point.

"Why you rushing me? You got other bitches coming through?" She gave him a cold killer stare with a prettier face.

"Yeah, a four hundred pound bitch with a fake leg."

"Boy whatever but if I had a fake leg, would you still eat my pussy the way you do?" She wanted to know because one of her friends has a fake leg and cries about how she never got her pussy ate. She cries about how niggas only want to hit her from the back.

"It depends if you rocking the fake leg or not at the moment."

"Oh, that's wrong."

"I'm saying. Half of a leg looks weird especially when the little nubb moves," he said, making her tear up while laughing.

The knock at the door startled both of them as Alina threw a sheet over her naked body and covering Lil Smoke.

"Who dat, bruh?" Lil Smoke saw Nafee come inside the room, eating chicken from KFC.

"Daddy called me today..." Nafee paused, not knowing Alina was even there because him and Emma been in his room all night. "Hey Alina."

"What's up, Nafee," Alina replied.

"What he say? Is he still mad we moved?"

"A little but he wants to meet Alina and Emma at Jummah."

"Huh, how he know about ... Better yet, I know you got a big mouth. So, forget it," Lil Smoke said.

"What's Jummah?" Alina was lost.

"Muslim service that we go to on Fridays," Nafee explained.

"Friday, I got two exams," Alina said.

"I guess we can't make it." Lil Smoke smiled.

"You will burn in hell, then." Nafee slammed the door behind him. He was upset Lil Smoke wasn't taking the religion as serious as him or Yasir.

"What your brother get upset for, baby?" She wondered.

"I believe in Allah and I'm a Muslim, but I live a life of sin. If I go to Jummah, praying and acting like a good Muslim, I won't feel right knowing I'ma sin an hour later," Lil Smoke confessed his deep feelings on why he don't be on his deen so hard. Nafee prayed five times a day and fasted every Ramadan.

"Allah forgives just like God?" She didn't know much about Muslims except for the clothes they wore.

"God is Allah in Arabic and yes he does forgive. I just don't know how much if I keep doing the same shit over and over."

"Maybe you should pray and go to Jummah then."

"I might but we got to get you back to school."

"I got my brother Wraith. I'll get there fast," she said as Lil Smoke was going to ask about him, but he put it to the side for now.

Chapter 36
Norwood, Miami

Hira arrived home an hour before her husband got home so she could prepare dinner and do some cleaning This was her normal routine. Since being a housewife the whole marriage, working a nine to five wasn't a part of her lifestyle.

Yasir wouldn't dare let her work anywhere. He wanted Hira to live a fabulous lifestyle and didn't have to move a muscle. He loved being the provider.

With so much free time on her hands, she would go to shop, martial art classes, and sometimes she loved going out walking enjoying the air. Hira was very talented in fighting but as she got older, her dreams of being a teacher in martial arts faded.

Hira entered her home with two shopping bags, taking off her shoes but leaving on the female Islamic garment she wore that covered the body. It was part of Hira's born religion. She forgot to send money back home to her country, but her brothers and sisters could wait until tomorrow.

She wondered what Lil Smoke and Nafee was up to. She hadn't saw them in weeks, but Yasir told her they supposed to come down to Jummah service Friday so that made Hira's day.

Since being in Nafee and Lil Smoke's life, she treated them like her own because they had no mother figure present. Not too many people knew but Hira couldn't have kids. That was a main reason she loved Nafee and Lil Smoke so much.

Inside the kitchen, Hira placed the bags of food on the counter but feeling something awkward, she paused.

"Nice to meet you," Hira said to the shadow behind the kitchen door.

"I would say the same." Khadija came from behind the kitchen door.

"Who are you supposed to be?" Hira showed no sign of fear as she started to unpack the food bag.

"Your worst nightmare or at least the bitch that's going to kill you."

"Since when does African assassins use guns?" Hira questioned, knowing the strong accent had to be from the motherland.

"I just like the way it looks in my hand, but I wouldn't waste a bullet on you," says Khadija cold bloodedly.

"Why waste time?" Hira unwrapped herself and got in fighting stance.

Khadija tossed the gun and leaped at Hira, swinging a nice combo. Hira ducked like a pro fighter, coming back at her with an uppercut that stumbled Khadija, taking her by shock.

"Okay, bitch. Let's go." Khadija wiped the blood from her lip.

Hira saw Khadija about to swing another left hook, so she ducked to only get a knee to the chin, knocking her backwards. Khadija hit Hira with a roundhouse kick to the sink.

Khadija continued to come but Hira grabbed a pan and smashed it in Khadija's face, almost knocking her opponent clean out.

Hira rushed her about to finish the job, but Khadija was a step ahead. She pulled out a blade and shoved it in Hira's heart repeatedly until Hira's body got stiff.

"Dumb bitch," Khadija said, looking for the biggest knife in the kitchen so she could cut out Hira's eyes, tongue, lips, and ears. That was the ultimate sign of disrespect in Africa after killing a person, to desecrate the body.

***

Khadija couldn't lie. She couldn't remember the last fight she had that could top Hira, but Khadija knew this already before coming through Hira's side door hours ago to wait on her.

The day Khadija saw Yasir show up to her home to fix the sink, she knew his face was familiar but at the moment, couldn't recall where she saw him.

After weeks of trying to figure it out, one day in her sleep, it all came back into her brain.

Yasir used to be one of Savage and Bama security guards at the mosque daily and he used to bring his wife, Hira there. Khadija continued to dig deep and found out they raised Lil Smoke and another child, Nafee.

Once having all the solid info, Khadija made her move which was today. Driving pass a cop car speeding, she didn't see when the detective snuck behind her, flashing his lights.

"Damn it!" Khadija shouted because she still had blood on her shirt, hands, and a busted up face as if she was just in a deadly car crash. Pulling next to a post office, she came up with a quick story tell the officer a friend of hers beat her ass because she just got caught having sex with her boyfriend.

The officer approached Khadija's car in a fast pace with an angry face. He was an old white man. Racist was written all over his face.

"You were going pretty fast there, little lady. Wow, what the hell happened to you?" The officer said, seeing Khadija's full bloody face with cuts and bruises.

"I was caught fucking my friend boyfriend and we got into a fight but I'm fine, officer, really."

"You don't look like it, Ms."

"Trust me, I had worse ass whipping than this." she smiled, laughing. The cop's face was still hardened.

"I think you need medical attention," he said, looking deeper into her face and car at the same time.

"Not really. I'll just take my ticket and leave if possible. " Khadija saw him looking over into her passenger seat. When she looked to her right, the weapon she was going to use to kill Hira was laid on the seat.

"Ms., get the fuck out the car with your hands up!" The cop yelled pulling out his Glock 17 and aiming it at her.

"Okay, relax." she did as he asked.

"Who you going to kill with that?" He questioned Khadija as she slowly got out of the car.

"Nobody sir, I swear." Khadija now stood outside the driver door.

"Turn around so I can pat you down." The cop told her, using one hand for his walkie talkie to call it in.

Khadija slowly turned around and slipped a blade out of her right sleeve and slashed the officer's neck as blood squirted on his uniform.

Once the body collapsed, she hoped back in the car and raced off.

Chapter 37
Norwood, Miami

Yasir had a long day at work, but he was happy to be off and heading home to his beautiful wife. She would be in the kitchen cooking by now. Every day before he arrived home, Hira would have a full meal ready for him.

Driving past the post office, Yasir saw a gang of cop cars, ambulances and the local news recording the scene as if something big happened.

"What the hell happened out here?" He mumbled to himself as police did checkpoints, stopping every car in front of him.

When it was Yasir's turn, he grabbed his ID and registration info, rolling down his window.

"Good evening, officer."

"How you doing? I just need to see your license. It's a random check point, sir," the older black cop stated.

"No problem, here you go." Yasir handed over his license.

"Okay, you're good to go, sir. Enjoy your day."

"If you don't mind me asking, what happened over there?" Yasir looked towards the commotion.

"An officer was brutally murdered with a knife. I never seen anything like it. Even though he was a piece of shit cop, he was still one of ours." The officer looked behind him, thankful it wasn't him.

"They found the killer?"

"No, that's why we're doing checkpoints all over the city. A witness said they saw a black, dark skinned pretty woman kill him and jump back in her car, speeding off." The cop shook his head.

"Well, good luck."

"Thank you," the cop repeated, going back to his job.

Yasir knew a woman couldn't be capable of committing that type of crime unless it was Hira, but his baby was far from dark skin or violent these days.

Pulling up home, he saw his baby girl car parked in the front. He grabbed all his tools and went inside. Yasir walked in the clean house, calling his wife, and wondering why he didn't smell food.

Hira would have the whole crib smelling like Halal food but today there were no scent, except a weird one Yasir was to use to.

"Hira, you in the kitchen?" yelled Yasir, only to see Hira laid in a puddle of blood with her eyes, lips, ears all sitting next to her head in a line.

Tears formed in Yasir's eyes as he hit the ground, picking up her lifeless head holding her like a baby.

"Allah, not her pleassee!" He screamed at the top of his lungs, unable to hold himself back. Yasir cried for twenty five minutes before he called the police, who made it to his home minutes later to conduct the horrible crime scene.

***

Miami University Hospital

KVon got off on the sixth floor with flowers and a teddy bear in his hand, making his way to room 621 at the end of the hallway.

Twice a week, KVon been making this same trip to see his niece, who was fighting a Cancer battle for the last six months. Today was her release day after finally beating Cancer at the young age of eighteen years old.

When KVon's brother was killed, he took it upon himself to take care of all his late brother's children. When Flaver was diagnosed with Cancer, KVon placed her in the best hospital, around the best doctors.

"Uncle KVon." Flaver smiled, seeing her uncle enter with the gifts while a nurse prepared Flaver's bag to be sent home with KVon.

"Hey beautiful, you ready to go home?" KVon asked, rubbing the scruff covering Flaver's bald head. Before Flaver's treatment, she had long dreads that hung down to the crack of her ass.

Even with a bald head, Flaver was still beautiful and sexy, even though she didn't feel like it no more.

"Yes, I been ready." Flaver let the nurse and KVon place her in a wheelchair.

"You hungry?" KVon asked, already having a big fest planned for her at home. It was a welcome home surprise party with family and her friends.

"I want some Creole food and FuFu," she shot back as the nurse laughed because she was the one who put Flaver on to FuFu, which was a part of her African culture.

"What the hell is that?" KVon knew it wasn't Haitian food unless it was some new shit.

"I'll tell you about it later." Flaver looked back at the nurse pushing her wheelchair and gave the African woman a wink.

KVon signed the release papers and made his way out to his truck, placing his niece in the front seat as she requested.

"When you get this?" Flaver liked the new BMW SU. It had everything in it.

"This is yours, baby girl."

"Oh, my God. Really?" She was excited.

"Yep, once you heal back up, you're going back to college in style to Atlanta." KVon saw how happy she was and couldn't help but smile.

Flaver attended Clark University in Atlanta before she came back for her father's funeral. She was diagnosed with Cancer right after. Life felt like a turmoil for her.

"Thank you so much." Flaver got emotional and started crying, something she rarely did but being overwhelmed did it. Plus, she had just beat Cancer.

"Don't cry, baby. You deserve it."

"I know." Flaver got herself together and started talked to talk about KVon's son, getting deep in a conversation.

KVon was about to make a left onto an expressway but a car slammed into the right passenger side, making the airbags blow up in his and Flaver's face.

By the time KVon was able to see, three gunmen with assault rifles it was too late.

Tat ... Tat ... Tat ... Tat ... Tat ...Tat ... Tat ... Tat ... Tat ...

KVon smashed the gas, busting a U-turn in the middle of the street as bullets still rattled the SUV. Looking over to Flaver, blood was pouring out of four holes in her face as Flaver's body was stiff with her eyes closed.

"No, baby girl!" KVon screamed, racing to the hospital but deep down, he could tell she was dead. Once at the hospital, Flaver was pronounced dead on arrival. KVon cried for hours at the hospital, unable to move.

Chapter 38
North Shore, Miami

Nafee and Lil Smoke got out of the car, walking into the house they both grew up in. They were sad and hurt over Hira's death.

When Nafee got the call, he told Lil Smoke and they knew it was time to go from Dr. Akbar's house so the duo could be enlightened on what took place.

Walking into the house, Yasir sat on the living room couch in a bad condition. He was incapable of moving or even talking.

"Assalaamalaikum," Nafee greeted his father to get nothing back.

"Give him time to grieve," Lil Smoke said, using a walker to walk off until Yasir finally spoke.

"Sit down … both of you," Yasir said without looking at them, focusing on an old picture of his Hira on their honeymoon.

Nafee and Lil Smoke both followed orders and sat down quietly, not saying a word.

"Someone took my wife, my other half, my soulmate, my heart and they will pay with their lives. There is a side to me I neglected so I can be a good father, role model, and husband. Killing is sometimes necessary and this is that time. I was able to put it together why the two of you moved out and its okay but know the rules before you play in the game. I love y'all. Now, give me time to mourn and y'all try not to get killed because I refuse to bury two loved ones back-to-back," Yasir said, now looking into their eyes with his cold stare.

Nafee and Lil Smoke both gave Yasir a hug even though Lil Smoke had a little trouble hugging him because his shit bag was in the way, but Yasir moved it over for him, smiling.

"I can't believe this shit. You think Yasir knows who did it?" Lil Smoke asked, getting back into the car, and seeing a missed call from Mucho.

"Maybe. We will find out soon, but I hope my dad don't go crazy. I saw him kill two people when he picked me up from daycare a long time ago. These two Mexicans ran down on him and he killed both of them, then asked me what I ate for lunch" Nafee said, laughing.

"I remember when Yasir was the Imom at that mosque in North Miami. One day, I popped up and saw him choke out the owner and drag him into the closet." Lil Smoke remembered that day like yesterday.

"That's probably why they shut that mosque down, bro."

"I wouldn't doubt it, dawgs," Lil Smoke said, reading a text from Mucho asking him to come by tomorrow for dinner. As bad as Lil Smoke wanted to say no, he couldn't because business came first.

"Lil Trap said Bowy got something for us," Nafee said, still thinking about poor Hira. He just hope she ain't get caught up in their dumb shit.

"I just want to get some sleep and take this shit bag off me, tonight."

"Facts. That thing looks weird. I pray I don't never get shot," Nafee stated.

"Keep fucking with me, you going to need two of these bitches," Lil Smoke said as they made it home quick.

It took Lil Smoke almost twenty minutes to get inside the apartment and when they walked inside, Emma was right there on the couch.

"Hey guys, where y'all been … Oh my God, Lil Smoke are you okay? Do you need help?" Emma jumped up with her pretty manicured feet out. Lil Smoke mind flashed to what Dr. Akbar said about an African wanted to kill him as he looked at Emma but as fast as the thought came, it left. The woman killed his brother ten years ago and Emma would've been too young.

"No, I'm good. I just need to rest but thanks." Lil Smoke saw her sad face as he walked to his room.

"Why he don't like me, baby?" Emma asked Nafee because she was a joyful high spirit person and hated when people disliked her.

"He just got to get used to you. We got a lot going on right now."

"Can I help?" She asked, hugging him.

"What ... hell no, you can't."

"Just asking but I got a job." She boasted, jumping up and down for her first job.

"Hold up, you got a job?" Nafee was surprised because all she wanted to do is shop, fuck, sleep, and go out.

"Yes, because I don't want to live off you, Nafee. I want to show you and Smoke that I'm not a lazy bitch or gold digger," she said.

"Babe, if I thought you were all that, I would've kept you in the friend zone."

"I guess you're right but this my first job. I'm geeked about it."

"Where?"

"A medical center near the college. One of the people I met worked there and hooked me up with a job," Emma said.

"I'm proud of you." Nafee kissed her and Lil Trap walked into the crib like he owned it.

"Where he at?" Lil Trap asked.

"In da back."

"Hey Trappy?" Emma said, calling him by the nickname she had for him.

"She's still here," Lil Trap said, walking to the back to see Lil Smoke trying to get comfortable in his big bed.

"Nigga, I see you don't know how to knock," Lil Smoke said.

"For what?"

"Next time, I'ma have my dick all out then, hoe ass nigga," Lil Smoke joked.

"Aight, bitch ass nigga, but peep this though, bruh. Bowy killed Big Worm and got some good info about KVon," Lil Trap said.

"Aight cool, but these pain meds kicking my ass. Pull up on me tomorrow once I get back from dinner with the plug."

"Damn, it's time to re-up already?"

"Nah, not yet. He just request me to be there."

"Aight cuz, but Alina came by twice looking for you. I told her you was out of town, but the bitch wasn't buying it at all. She felt your ass got shot," Lil Trap joked.

"Bro, get the fuck out." Lil Smoke got under his covers, knowing his boy wanted to joke and get a few good laughs off him.

"I'll be back in the morning, hoe." Lil Trap closed the door, forgetting to tell his boy Solana just lost her parents.

Lil Trap went to interrupt Nafee and Emma's cuddle session. Emma didn't like Lil Trap at times, and tonight, she had no problem showing it when she cursed him out for turning the TV. This was the first time Nafee heard her curse and couldn't believe it.

Lil Smoke took an Uber to Mucho's crib to see a few big bodyguards walking around after they let him inside.

"Lil Smoke, how you doing? You're right in time for dinner. Sit down, my friend. You look hurt," Mucho said, sitting at the head of the expensive dining room table. He was next to Lura, who wore a Fendi dress looking very classy.

"I'm okay. I ran into a little problem, but the rest is being handled." Lil Smoke said, seeing how beautiful Lura was looking but tried to control his stares.

"Thanks for coming. I just felt like it would be only right to invite you to a meal with us. Me and Lura both be so busy we don't even do shit like this anymore," Mucho said, seeing the food come out.

"What happened to you?" Lura asked, not letting go

"Nothing much," he lied, seeing she was getting up. Lura walked over to him and tapped his side and he flinched in pain.

"Who shot you?" Lura was upset.

"I took care of it. One dude is already dead. I got one left"

"Lil Smoke, we got people on standby for shootings and killings," Mucho said.

"I know but I'll be able to handle my own beef."

"This is a family. Your beef is ours," Mucho said, seeing Lura was so upset she excused herself from the dinner table.

"She okay?" Lil Smoke asked.

"Lura is on her period, and she don't like to see her family hurt and neither do I. You say you got it under control, so I believe you. Now, let's eat up," Mucho spoke.

Chapter 39
Pork N Beans PJs, Miami

It only took a week for Rakeem to flip Pork N Bean projects. It was Jiam's old turf but was his now that he got the problem out of the way.

When the word landed Rakeem killed Jiam, the hood saluted Rakeem because nobody else had the balls to kill him.

Everybody who worked for Jiam, now worked for him and he loved the feeling of having one of the most profitable books in Miami under his wing.

Coming fresh home from a home invasion and gun charge, Rakeem wanted to get money so when he ran into Nafee in the mosque, they started talking one thing led to another.

Nafee told him he would introduce him to the crew sometime this week when shit died down, but he was a part of their team now.

Rakeem was medium height, palm tree dreads, dark skin, tattoos on face, beard, and gold teeth. He was a true Florida boy.

"Ayo, Rakeem," an older cat named Choice said, getting out of his car in the back of the building, which was a hang out area.

"What's up, Choice?" Rakeem knew the old head used to be a serious killer back in the day. They say Choice lost his kids and wife in a big shootout. Then, he got locked up. Word on the street was when Choice got arrested, he picked up a new habit, sniffing dope.

"Welcome home, youngster," Choice stated.

"Thanks. How you been?" Rakeem saw Choice looked clean and glowing.

"Ain't shit. I live in Broward County now. I'm out there trying to make some paper," Choice said proudly.

"That's what's up, bruh."

"I heard what happened to that rat ass Jiam nigga," Choice said.

"You know he was a snitch too, huh?"

"That little bitch told on me when he was only sixteen for a murder I beat," Choice said, thinking back to when Jiam took the stand on him in the court room.

"He got my brother so much time, this nigga don't even know who he is no more, bruh." Rakeem hated the fact his brother wouldn't see day light again because of rats.

"Sorry to hear that but living in these streets, we take risks. Niggas forget about shit. The game ain't all peaches and cream. I beat five murders in my lifetime and did fifteen years for one. I lost my whole family, beefing with Big Zoe and them Zoe pounds before that Savage kid took care of them. What I'm saying is, this shit ain't for the weak minded or weak hearted," Choice said, speaking real shit.

"I feel you, big bruh."

"I've heard you're the man out here, now," Choice spoke.

"Yeah, you can say that Choice. Why, what happened?"

"Maybe we can get some money together. I'm making big moves in Broward County."

"Choice, no disrespect but I'ma keep it real with you, my nigga. I heard you was down bad on that dog food."

"I was fucked up thug when I lost my family. My life fell apart but I'm not that same man. I've overcome my struggles and become who I am today," Choice told him.

"If I fuck with you, how I know you won't relapse, bruh?"

"Never judge a man off his past but by his actions that your eyes can see. I'm on a paper chase," Choice spoke.

"That's law, bruh. I've known you to be a supreme hustler out here. I remember you was the first nigga to come through in a Cadillac sitting on dem things."

"That was the old days. You was a little nigga then, thug," Choice said smiling and reminiscing.

Rakeem and Choice talked for a half hour before Rakeem agreed to put Choice on when he got his next order.

***

Bowy's grandma, Andreina and his little sister, Karmen were coming home from shopping at the mall for Karmen's upcoming birthday party she planned to have at the house.

"Grandma?" Karmen said, driving down their block where they lived.

"Yes, love?" Andreina drove her new luxury truck that Bowy recently brought her.

"How have we been getting all this money, especially since mommy died." Karmen missed her mom, who she had to bury yesterday.

"God blessed us baby," Andreina said, not wanting to tell her grandbaby the truth.

"Okay I guess."

"No worries. You going to be okay. God got the whole family," Andreina said, pulling into her small driveway. She was still emotional about her daughter funeral yesterday.

"I'll bring the bags in," Karmen said, getting out and opening the backdoor tired from a long day of shopping.

When Karmen and Andreina walked toward the front, two gunmen jumped out of the bushes on them with AK-47 assault rifles.

Tat, Tat, Tat, Tat, Tat, Tat, Tat, Tat, Tat, Tat, Tat, Tat, Tat, Tat, Tat, Tat …

KVon's gunmen ran off to their getaway car, knowing the two women KVon paid them twenty thousand for was dead.

***

Bowy was with his side bitch to drop off his sister an early birthday gift, which was some diamond earrings and a Chanel bag. She always talked it about because a few girls had it in her high school.

Having to bury his mom took a lot out of Bowy's young heart but he knew it came with the game and death was a part of life.

Since getting his bag up, he knew taking care of his family was first. His uncles used to always tell him a real man takes care of his loved ones, family, and friends.

"Babe, look at this shit." Bowy's girl said, seeing blue and red lights all over the place as people were all outside.

"Maybe a car accident but my grandma lives right there," Bowy said, sliding her his gun he had on his lap. She placed the gun in her purse he brought, already knowing what time it was.

"Damn babe, that shit looks crazy," she said.

"What the fuck?" Bowy parked the car when he saw cops running in and out his grandma's crib in white outfits.

"Ayo officer!" Bowy yelled to one of the cops, who was placing caution tape around the block.

"Sir, you can't cross this."

"Man, fuck all that, bruh. Why are y'all running in and out my grandma house?" Bowy yelled, trying to look over the tall man.

"Your grandma is Andreina?" The cop asked.

Bowy got antsy. The cop even knew her name.

"Yes, what the fuck is going on?" Bowy saw two white body bags get pulled out by an EMT.

"We need you over here, sir. Your grandma was murdered with another young woman, who could be her daughter or granddaughter. Could you follow me?" The cop said, letting him through the ropes.

Bowy felt like his soul was leaving his body as he got closer to see his grandma and little sister's bodies filled with bullet holes, laying in pools of blood.

"I'm Captain Smitty from downtown. Can we ask you a few questions?" An officer said with a notepad and pen ready to take notes.

"Are you fucking serious?" Get the fuck out my face, bitch ass nigga," Bowy said, walking off with tears in his eyes. He was pissed. All the cops looked at each other, knowing it was about to be another cold case.

Chapter 40
Northshore, Miami

Yasir sat in his living room with the lights off, in deep thought, waiting on Lil Smoke to come because he needed to speak with him.

Burying Hira yesterday took a lot out of him, but he was glad how the Islamic funeral came out. Not too many people arrived, just close friends and some of Hira's family from Morocco.

This morning, Yasir managed to put some things together and he knew who killed his wife. It was Khadija, the woman who killed Savage. Putting everything together, he knew Lil Smoke could be in danger.

He heard keys and someone entering the house.

"Pops!" Lil Smoke yelled.

"Living room."

"Damn, what you a vampire now? It's dark as hell in here." Lil Smoke turned on the living room lights, almost falling over some shoes.

"I need to speak to you. Have a seat." Yasir hated talking about Savage's death. He tried to put it behind him.

"What's up, you good?" Lil Smoke asked, knowing Yasir was fucked up emotionally after Hira's funeral yesterday.

"I know who killed my wife"

"Who, and how did you find out so fast?" Lil Smoke asked.

"The same person who killed my wife, killed your brother."

"Shit!" Lil Smoke shouted, knowing the assassin bitch was starting to close in on him.

"She remembered Hira from the mosque and killed her, so I figured you and me could be next on the lady's hit list," Yasir stated.

"Let that hoe come. I got a lot of rounds waiting on her."

"You don't get it. She is a trained killer. You won't see her coming. The same bullet shells found around Savage was found around her husband, Bama," Yasir told him.

"She killed her own husband?" Lil Smoke met some cold-blooded people, but she was ice cold.

"Yes, and I got a feeling that she'll come for you." Yasir looked worried.

Lil Smoke didn't want to tell Yasir that he already knew about the woman. He just listened and played along.

"I want you and Nafee to go out of town for a few weeks until I get this figured out."

"A few weeks?" Lil Smoke repeated, not trying to hear that.

"Please. Just for a little bit. A couple of days, that's all I need," Yasir begged.

"Five days."

"Seven."

"Six." Lil Smoke tried to bargain with him.

"Okay, fair. I just want the both of you to be safe."

"Pops, we'll be fine."

"I believe you but I'm not going to see my own kids six feet deep," Yasir stated

"I'ma call you when we get back," Lil Smoke said leaving.

"Where y'all going? Los Angeles or New York. I know the both of you used to always talk about traveling to those cities.

"Atlanta," Lil Smoke said

"Your brother had some people out there from back in the day but be safe," Yasir stated before seeing him leave.

***

Downtown, Atlanta

Lil Smoke, Alina, Nafee, and Emma all came out to Atlanta for a week to get away from Miami.

Lil Trap and Bowy held down everything back home, but Lil Smoke made it clear not to make any big moves without his presence.

"This going to be so fun," Emma said, pumped up about going to Magic City.

"It's going to be a lot of ass in there. I hope y'all can manage," Lil Smoke said looking at Alina, knowing she had a jealous flaw.

"I'm trying slap some ass myself," Alina joked as they walked out of the hotel to climb in his Bentley SUV that he drove out there.

"How long we out here for?" Nafee asked in a low pitch voice.

"A week, bruh, just chill. We going to let Yasir do him and we'll finish up whatever he don't," Lil Smoke said.

"Aight."

"I love it out here, babe," Emma spoke.

"We need to go shopping here," Alina said.

"I'm all for that one," Emma said, happy to take a week off work to chill with her boo.

"Who money y'all spending?" Lil Smoke asked them both before climbing into the truck.

"Yours," Alina shot back.

The club wasn't far from the hotel and when they arrived, it was packed with no parking spaces except one. Six men were blocking it off as if someone famous was about to arrive.

"This shit popping," Nafee said, looking around for a parking spot.

"Hell yeah, wow," Alina followed.

"Spot right," Emma said, pointing at a Porsche pulling out of a spot.

"Perfect," Lil Smoke spoke, parking and ready to blow a few bands.

Inside the club, Lil Smoke tried to pay for a VIP section, but they were all taken, so the crew found a spot on the wall in a corner.

"Bitches flying down from the ceiling and shit," Nafee said as three chicks with big asses pulled up in front of them and started to twerk.

Alina and Emma tossed money and turned up.

"I'ma go order some bottles," Lil Smoke announced, walking off happy to see his girl having fun. He even thought about asking about a threesome tonight.

At the bar, Lil Smoke bumped into a man and by a mistake spilled the man's drink on him.

"What the fuck, my nigga?" The dude said, spilling his cup of Dusse all over his white LV outfit.

"My bad, bruh," Lil Smoke said, not seeing thirty niggas surround him.

"I ain't even tripping, bruh … Yo, Vice, go get me a new shirt!" The man yelled to one of his soldiers as Lil Smoke saw almost half the club was on him.

"I'll pay for that bro," Lil Smoke said.

"It's cool, dog. Where you from?"

"Miami."

"Okay, I had some real solid niggas out there a while back."

"That's what's up," Lil Smoke replied.

"I just got up in here but my VIP in over there. You're welcome to come. Miami niggas is always good in my city because if it wasn't for my nigga, Savage, I wouldn't be me."

"Savage?"

"Yeah, you heard of him?" The man took off his shirt and his worker handed him a Versace shirt.

"That's my brother. May Allah bless his soul."

"Ain't no fucking way. Hold on, your name –"

"Lil Smoke. That's me."

"This is big. I'm Lil D. I'm a powerful cousin. I took over the city when he got killed. When Savage got killed, I found a new Miami plug and been the richest nigga in my city. I run Atlanta," Lil D said.

"I'm making big moves in Miami. We need to link."

"Fo' sho. Come up to the VIP. You family," Lil D said as Lil Smoke went to get everybody and slid to Lil D VIP.

Chapter 41
Torrean, Mexico

Preslee placed her father inside the truck with four security guards as they had to go to a local hospital because he was feeling very sick tonight.

"I forgot my purse. I'll be right back." Preslee rushed up the stairs, going to her room for a purse.

Tat, Tat, Tat, Tat, Tat, Tat, Tat, Tat, Tat …

Preslee heard shooting outside. She grabbed a SK assault rifle and rushed out front to see eight shooters going against her men, but she took them by surprise.

Tat, Tat, Tat, Tat, Tat, Tat, Tat, Tat, Tat, Tat, Tat, Tat …

She killed four of the gunmen and her guards shot two as one ran off, tossing his empty weapon. Preslee shot the last gunman and saw it don't put him out. She ran up to the man lying on the ground, already pleading for his life.

"Who the fuck sent you here?" Preslee stood over his face with her weapon pointed at the gunman's nose.

"Royal," he said in perfect English.

Tat, Tat, Tat, Tat, Tat …

She didn't need to hear nothing else as Preslee gladly killed him. She looked to see two of her men dead.

Preslee forgot all about her dad inside the truck, fighting for his life. She rushed and opened the door to see his old frail body slumped and filled with bullet holes. "Daddyyyy … Help …" Preslee screamed at the top of her lungs.

The house nurse came out to try and save the cartel boss, but he was gone. Preslee held her father for twenty minutes in her arms, crying the whole time.

***

Palm City County, Miami

Khadija packed up a duffle bag with clothes for her trip to Texas in the morning. There was something important she had to take care of out there.

She had to pay a friend in Brownsville, TX a special visit that's been well past due.

The last time she saw Emma with her target, Khadija needed a minute to really put a better plan together. Her sister spoke of having a boyfriend many times, but Khadija never really paid it no mind and now she wished she did.

How hard could it really be to kill a teenager was the only thing that played in the back of Khadija's head. She knew if Lil Smoke was anything like Smoke, she would have a big problem.

She went to the kitchen, still dressed in her jogging suit because Khadija just got back from her hour run. She tried to stay loyal to 5-6 days a week.

Grabbing a bottle of Gatorade out the fridge, she started to feel someone was behind her. She turned around to see Yasir pointing a gun at her. Khadija laughed at him.

"You find death funny, I see," Yasir said, inching a little closer.

"It took you this long to put it all together. Don't feel bad because when you first came by, the thought went through my mind as to who you were," Khadija said.

"You killed my friends and wife."

"Yes, I did but more so business, never personal."

"Why?"

"I took a contract from a Haitian man named Big Zoe for Savage's death and his crew were a bonus because I hated them," she told him, seeing he was getting too close.

"You killed my wife. Why? She was a good Muslim woman, you bitch."

"She was to catch your attention so I could get you, then Lil Smoke."

"Well, look how them tables turns," Yasir said

"Not really, Yasir because I fear nothing," Khadija told him before swiftly disarming him at the speed of lighting. Yasir tried to let off a shot but couldn't. She was too fast.

Once his gun was tossed, he flung himself at Khadija, trying to attack her but she sidestepped and kicked him twice in the side of his face.

Yasir couldn't believe how powerful her kick was. He was pissed now.

"Bring it, little bitch. I'ma teach you something." Yasir swung at her but missed.

Khadija moved quick on her feet, and he couldn't keep up.

She hit him with a four piece combo before kicking Yasir into the sink, where he picked up a knife.

He swung the knife in her direction, but Khadija backed up, ducking him. She did a roundhouse kick to his temple, putting him out as he dropped the knife.

Feeling a little dizzy, Yasir got up, wanting more.

"Come on," Yasir said, punching Khadija in her face with a power blow almost knocking the daylight out of her.

"That's all you got," Khadija said, spitting out blood.

Yasir threw a few haymakers, but she bobbed and weaved, coming up with two uppercuts and a left hook, stumbling him. Khadija hit the big man with a front kick. This time, he went to sleep, collapsing on the marble floor near the gun.

Khadija was winded while looking at Yasir sleep on the floor.

"I won't kill you because I want you awake next time," Khadija said, spitting on him and running upstairs to get her duffle bag.

Leaving him dead in the house she had in her name, would've been bad so leaving Yasir sleep was her best bet.

***

Dade County, Miami
Days later

Royal was in his living room, painting a masterpiece, something he loved to do in his free time. He felt like he never had any.

Sending his goons to kill Preslee and her dad took some balls but he grew them. He figured if the Torreon Cartel was out the way, he could convince the other Cartels to buy from him, leaving them no option. When one of the gunmen came back saying Preslee was alive, he regretted the hit because she was supposed to be the main target.

The front door opened, and he knew who it was. Only one other person had the keys.

"Alina," Royal called his little sister's name.

"Hey, Randolph," she called him by his government.

"Where you been? I missed you, lil sis."

"School and living a happy life. Nice painting," she said, walking into the fancy living room.

"I want to take you out tomorrow," Royal said

"Okay, I'm just tired so I'ma get some rest but tomorrow I'm down. Sister and brother day and please, none of your goons," she said.

"Maybe. Things are a little shaky right now."

"I don't care. No goons or I'm not going."

"Your just like mommy." Royal remembered their mom used to tell their dad Montanta the same thing when traveling places.

Chapter 42
University Hospital, Miami

Lil Smoke and Nafee stood outside of Yasir's hospital room, looking at him wrapped up like a mummy. The doctor told them Yasir drove himself to the hospital and passed out in the lobby.

When the doctor explained how lucky Yasir was to arrive the time he did because a few minutes later, the blood clots that were forming in his head could have killed him.

Nafee asked what happened and the doctor went to tell him how someone injured Yasir's cranium, mandible, broke his jaw, the cervical spine, lumbar spine, ligament, and a few cartilaginous joints.

The doc said the damage was equal to him fighting a gorilla on a bad day.

"Who the fuck did this?" Nafee asked himself, furious seeing his dad in a fucked up condition.

"There is something that I need to tell you." Lil Smoke promised Yasir he wouldn't, but Lil Smoke felt like he had to.

"What's that?"

"You remember when we just went to Atlanta?"

"Of course."

"Well, it was Yasir's idea that we go," Lil Smoke said.

"Why? I don't get it."

"The person who killed Hira is the same person that killed Savage and Yasir put it all together. He begged me to get out of town for a week."

"And we come back to this. Why would you keep some shit like that from me, bro?" Nafee asked, feeling betrayed somewhat.

"I tried to respect pop's wishes but I ain't know this was going to happen, bruh."

"So, you telling me a bitch did all of this?"

"I guess."

"That's hard to believe. I'ma go clear my head. This shit too much." Nafee turned to walk off.

"I'ma come with you."

"No, please don't. You did enough," Nafee told him, leaving the hospital making Lil Smoke feel bad and sad.

Lil Smoke looked at Yasir one last time, trying to make more sense of how a chick can do this much damage on a big man like Yasir, who is over six feet.

He had to go handle some business because Lil Trap and Bowy were out on a big mission, and they would need his assistance.

***

Lake Lucerne Park, Miami

Lil KeeKee was running the football up and down the field in his number one jersey, scoring a touchdown against the Opalocka Hurricanes.

"Good job, KeeKee," the coach yelled as the game ended with Lil KeeKee's touchdown.

Twenty minutes later, Lil KeeKee walked out the park, waiting for his dad, who missed the whole game. Something he had been doing a lot.

"You KVon, boy?" a man asked, pulling up in a new Cadillac.

"Yeah," Lil KeeKee said in his kiddish voice.

"He sent me to pick you up. Get in," the man said, opening the passenger door from the inside of the car.

"You sure my dad sent you because I'm not supposed to get in the car with strangers," Lil KeeKee said.

"I'm family. Boy get in," the man who was Lil Trap told him before he climbed in.

"I scored five touchdowns, Mr." Lil KeeKee said.

"Wow, five?" Lil Trap said.

"Yep, it was easy too," Lil KeeKee bragged.

"You want to go get some ice cream and pizza?"

"Hell yeah."

"Okay, let's make it happen." Lil Trap took Lil KeeKee to North Miami for ice cream and pizza.

***

KVon arrived at Lake Lucerne Park, a little later, to pick up his son from his big football game that he missed.

Looking around, he saw only the football coach, placing equipment inside his truck.

"What's up, OG? Where my son?" KVon pulled up on the coach.

"KVon, you missed it. Little man scored five touchdowns today. I'm telling you that boy finna make it," the coach said.

"I already know. Where he at?" KVon said, looking around to see no kids.

"All the kids left. I thought that was you picking him up in that gray Cadillac."

"Grey Cadillac." KVon said, confused because his baby mother drove a Benz. She would've called first before picking Lil KeeKee up.

"Yeah, is everything okay?" The coach saw an awkward look appear on KVon.

"Yes, I'ma figure it out." KVon said, pulling off and hoping one of Lil KeeKee's friends' parents picked him up.

KVon pulled out his phone to call his baby mom but a blocked number popped up.

"Who dis?" KVon answered.

"Your worst fucking nightmare. Bowy, you bitch ass nigga. We got your son," Bowy said.

"If you touch him, I'll –"

"You will what, nigga? I have no family left. You took everybody I love. Now, it's your turn."

"What you want?"

"You exchanged for little man. Meet us at the bridge in Liberty City at 11pm. Don't be late, hoe ass nigga," Bowy said before hanging up.

KVon's mind went crazy as he felt like his life was now shattering. KVon knew he couldn't let his son suffer for his mistake, so he knew what he had to do.

***

Liberty City, Miami

Hours later, Lil Smoke, Lil Trap, and Bowy posted up under a dark bridge for KVon's arrival.

Bowy had Lil KeeKee tied up in the back of his boy truck while Lil Smoke and Lil Trap leaned on the Bentley, enjoying the night heat.

"You good?" Lil Trap asked seeing something been bothering him.

"Yeah."

"Here he go," Lil Trap said, seeing a BMW come under the bridge with bright HD lights.

KVon parked and got out with his hands up, walking toward them and looking for his son.

"I'm all yours. Just let him go," KVon said.

"I call the shots, nigga but let me know something. Who you work for?" Lil Smoke asked.

"Royal someone you don't want to fuck with," says KVon.

"I'll deal with that later … Tell Bowy to let his son out," Lil Smoke told Lil Trap.

KVon saw Bowy snatch out his son from the back and threw him on the ground.

"What now?" KVon asked, seeing Bowy look like he wanted to chop his head off.

"You know what happens now," Lil Trap said as he lifted a gun at KVon. Not trying to go out like no sucker, KVon pulled a gun out his back side.

Bloc, Bloc, Bloc, Bloc, Bloc, Bloc, Bloc, Bloc, Bloc …

KVon's body fell on the ground, dropping his weapon as they lit his ass up for even thinking about trying some dumb shit.

When Lil Smoke turned around to tell Bowy to let the kid go, he heard gunfire. Bowy shot the little kid in his head.

"What the fuck, nigga? Why you kill the kid?" Lil Smoke was heated.

"They killed my little sister," Bowy replied.

"We don't kill kids, fool," Lil Smoke said.

"My bad," Bowy said as they left.

Romell Tukes

Chapter 43
Torreon, Mexico

Preslee buried her father behind their home where she grew up. Mucho was in the family room on Zoom, on a video call with some people from Cuba.

Now the Torreon Cartel belonged to her, which was a big task, but luckily since a little girl, her father showed her the ins and outs for days like this.

Royal played on her mind every night and she couldn't sleep or think straight knowing the man who killed her father was still out there somewhere.

"You okay, mami?" Mucho walked into the room with a cigar in his hand.

"Put that shit out. I hate that smoke," she said very moody. Mucho knew whenever she got like this somebody was gon' die.

"Your father smoked them all day."

"Yes, but you're not my father. Now, put it out and get ready to leave."

"What? I thought you wanted to chill here for a few more days," Mucho said.

"Why would I want to stay in the same house they killed my dad at, and I just buried him here?" She shouted.

"Okay baby, where you want to go?"

"I'm moving to Miami," she said, getting off the bed to pack up some important items to take.

"Move to Miami? When did you figure this out?"

"Does it matter?"

"No not really. I just want you to understand. You can't move off emotion no more, Preslee. You run a Cartel," Mucho said, following her into the closet.

"Emotions … The fucker who killed my father is probably out there on a beach somewhere and you talking about emotions."

"Not like that, Preslee."

"When I kill Royal and everything that he loves, we can talk about emotions. Didn't he just shoot you and get your mom killed?" She spat.

"Yes, and he he will pay when the time is right, but I don't react off emotion or impulse. I plot things out."

"Oh, so that's what you call it. I call it being a pussy." She looked at him, packing her things.

Mucho wanted to choke the shit out of her, but he knew Preslee was hurt and upset about losing her father.

Preslee saw him walk out and cursed at herself because she was mad. Mucho was her life but right now the only thing on her mind was to kill.

Moving to Miami was going to be a big risk because she had to relocate her goons and bring them with her because she planned to cause havoc.

***

Dade County, Miami

Alina spent the night in her old room at the mansion, but she had to go and take an exam in two hours.

She climbed out of bed, placing her feet in her Dior slippers, and walking downstairs to see if the maids made some food because she was starving.

Royal took her on his yacht yesterday and then shopping. She couldn't have had a better day, but she missed Lil Smoke dearly. Last night, she had a dream they was making love and woke to sticky sheets that she changed at 4am.

Today, she wanted to tell Royal about Lil Smoke, but she was a little nervous because Royal was very overprotective.

Walking into the kitchen, a maid was making eggs, pancakes, and pork sausages, Alina's favorite. She walked into the dining room to see Royal drinking liquor early in the morning, yelling to someone on the phone.

"I just lost millions. I don't give a fuck about KVon son. He ain't make me no money. I want you to find that Lil Trap and Lil

Smoke kid and kill them before they come kill us next. It's clear they don't respect the code, killing kids and shit. We can focus on Mucho and his people later, Jynx," Royal said, hanging up turning around to see Alina.

"You okay?" Alina asked, trying to act like she wasn't just eavesdropping on him.

"I'm fine, how was your sleep?" Royal asked, pouring himself a cup of strong Rum from the islands.

"I'm about to go back to school. I just wanted to say bye." Alina went in the kitchen, feeling her body get numb after hearing what Royal said about her man.

"You should let my guards take you back to school," Royal said entering the kitchen.

"I'm okay."

"I'm not asking you. I'm telling you, Alina."

"Okay."

Royal went upstairs and Alina went in the backyard to cry. She knew when Royal wanted someone, he would do whatever he can to achieve that.

She started to wonder what type of shit Lil Smoke was really into if he had the Cartel after him.

***

Carol City, Miami

Bowy, Lil Trap, Nafee, and Rakeem just got done playing a two on two basketball game, full court.

"I needed that cardio," Rakeem said, sitting down on the basketball court.

"Facts, bruh," Nafee added.

"We won both games." Lil Trap dapped Bowy, his partner.

"It's about to be a mean takeover now with KVon gone," Nafee said.

"I can't believe niggas got him out the way. KVon use to be a beast," Rakeem said. Today was his first time meeting Bowy and Lil Trap but he liked their vibes.

"There is always someone bigger and badder than the next. Even us, but right now, we got it," Lil Trap said.

"I heard a lot of good things about you, Rakeem. It's an honor to have you with the team thug," says Bowy.

"That's love, bruh. I'ma put on for us. I got niggas in Broward ready to lock it down. You feel me, bruh?" Rakeem said.

"We need to expand outside Dade County. That's good timing. Lil Smoke going to be happy to hear this," says Lil Trap.

"This weekend's going to be a new movie. Make sure that paper in order and I ain't counting all that shit," says Nafee.

"That's your job," Nafee recited.

"Shoot to kill." Lil Trap made everybody laugh.

"Let's get another game," Bowy said as he jumped up, ready to ball.

"I'm down." Rakeem took off his shirt, ready to hit the court.

"I got five bands on the next game," Lil Trap said as Bowy took the bet, but Nafee and Rakeem didn't gamble.

Chapter 44
Golden Beach, FL

Lil Smoke drove to Dr. Akbar's mansion to pay him a visit. He wanted to thank him and ask him a few questions. Pulling up into the wrap around driveway, he saw a waterfall in the center with a lion spitting water from his mouth.

"This nigga got money," Lil Smoke said to himself, getting out the Bentley. He saw a red Bugatti and a couple of other expensive luxury cars that he saw a few times in Miami.

Lil Smoke hadn't heard from Alina in days. He was starting to get a little worried, but he knew how she could act at times.

Before he made it to the door, it flew open. Lil Smoke saw Scarlit standing there with colorful eyes, curves that could be seen in her jeans and her exotic features.

"I saw you pull in on the monitors. How you doing?" Scarlet asked.

"Fine." Lil Smoke choked up.

"You heal well, I see."

"I try but I really want to thank you for helping me."

"Anytime, but my father is in his upstairs cave waiting on you. I have to go," Scarlit said, giving him a smile before leaving.

"What's your name?" Lil Smoke asked something he already knew just for more conversation.

"If you really want to know, you'll find out," Scarlit said, opening the door to a red Bugatti that was worth a million dollars.

"Okay, Scarlit."

"Yes, see," she said, climbing in the car. Lil Smoke walked inside, forgetting to ask her where Dr. Akbar's cave was.

"Lil Smoke comes upstairs. Nice to see you walking regularly," Dr. Akbar said from the upper level staircase.

"Thanks to you."

"What can I say? That's my life and it made me a millionaire."

"So, you got all this from being a doctor?" Lil Smoke said, walking upstairs.

"No, I own a lot of things. I'll just say that kid but come into my man cave." Dr. Akbar opened the French doors to his library.

"Damn, this shit huge."

"I love to read but have a seat. What's on your mind?"

"The man who raised me, Yasir, I feel like there is something about him that I can't see."

"Hold on, Yasir raised you? I thought you was raised by a kin to Britt." Dr. Akbar's face said so much.

"You know him?"

"Before Savage's death, he came and told me someone close to him wanted him dead and he went on to tell me it was a man named Yasir. Savage found out Yasir and a man they called Big Zoe was close friends and took a bounty to kill Savage. I guess Khadija beat him to the punch," Dr. Akbar explained.

"I guess this is why he's trying to kill Khadija?" It was all starting to make sense to him. The trip to Atlanta and the death of Hira.

"Yes, I can't believe your alive."

"Britt left me with him the last time I saw her."

"That explains it. She had no clue Yasir was plotting to kill him."

"Fuck, dawg." Lil Smoke's head started to hurt.

"There are a lot of questions and answers you have that will be brought to light sooner than later. Trust me."

"Thank you. I have to go," Lil Smoke said, getting up trying to understand it all without overloading his head.

"One last thing young man." Dr. Akbar stopped him at the door.

"Yeah?"

"Trust nobody."

"Better understood than said," Lil Smoke said before leaving.

***

South, Miami

Since losing their mother and father, Jynx and Solana had been spending a lot of time together. Today, they were going to get dolled up at a hair salon.

"You look nice," Jynx said, taking a look at Solana's off-white outfit.

"My man got it for me," Solana replied, looking at the beautiful palm trees and kids in the streets chasing down the ice cream truck.

"Boyfriend vibes."

"Yep."

"No wonder why I ain't start seeing you until mom and dad's funeral." Jynx said, hating bringing up her late mom and dad.

"They didn't have to do mommy and daddy like that," said Solana.

"I'ma find and handle it," Jynx said.

"How? You don't know the first thing about killing people," Solana told her.

Jynx forgot for a second that Solana knew nothing about her other life.

"I know people." Jynx made Solana laugh as a van pulled up to the driver's side.

Solana looked over at her sister to talk shit. She stopped at the red light to see a van door slide open. Mexicans hopped out with AK-47 assault rifles.

"Jynx watch out!" Solana yelled.

Tat, Tat, Tat, Tat, Tat, Tat, Tat, Tat, Tat, Tat, Tat …

Jynx laughed at the shooters as bullets only left scratches because she had the coupe bulletproofed last week.

She drove off calmly, seeing Solana look like she was about to have a heart attack.

"You straight, sis?" Jynx asked as Solana looked at her as if she was a crazy bitch.

"How the fuck did that just happen?" Solana asked.

"Magic. We riding in a Holy Ghost." Jynx smiled, knowing it had to be her enemy Lura trying to finish her, but Jynx was two steps ahead.

***

Miami Beach, Miami

Preslee and Lura both were in the kitchen, cooking and having a good time They were laughing and joking. Lura told Preslee everything she knew about Jynx and how she was down with Royal.

When Preslee heard about Jynx, she wanted her dead too. She sent some goons at Jynx just to greet her Cartel still.

Mucho walked into the kitchen and looked at both women, knowing shit was about to be all bad in Miami.

"Hey, babe," Preslee said.

"Y'all up to no good, huh?" Mucho says, smelling the good food.

"I thought you was sleep, ugly?" Lura asked to meet up with his clients out west.

"Me and Lura going to New York for the weekend," Preslee said.

"I don't even want to know why at all, but I love y'all and have a good day." Mucho left them talking. They were really plotting a move on Royal this weekend, not a trip to NYC.

Chapter 45
Northshore, Miami

Yasir had been feeling a little better since leaving the hospital after almost losing his life to Khadija.

He was on bedrest, but it was better than being in some hospital bed, smelling old dead people that was dying every hour.

Laying in the bed, he tried to come up with plans to kill Khadija before she came to find him because next time, he knew it wouldn't be too pretty by far.

Turning the TV, he didn't even see Lil Smoke standing there until it was too late.

"You startled me kid. When did you get here?" Yasir asked, happy to see him.

"I just got here," Lil Smoke said.

"You okay? Something looks like it's bothering you," Yasir told him, seeing he was moving funny.

"There is, Yasir." Lil Smoke walked into the room with a gun in his hand. Yasir saw the chrome pistol and took a deep breath.

"Who told you?" Asked Yasir, knowing it was time to reveal his darkest secrets.

"I think you have bigger problems." Lil Smoke cocked his gun.

"Growing up in Lil Haiti, I was poor. I had nothing, not a pot to piss in. When I met Big Zoe, my life changed. When I went to jail and became Muslim, I started to change my ways. But after coming home, Big Zoe made a way for me and for that I owed him loyalty. When Big Zoe asked me to get into Savage's circle to kill him, I did. Savage turned out to be a real good brother and it was hard for me to kill him. When he paid Khadija, I had no clue until after Big Zoe was killed by Britt. The day Khadija killed Savage, I felt the weight lifted off my shoulders because it was hard for me to pull the trigger," Yasir stated in deep thought.

"Why look after me?"

"I felt it was only right. You were a little kid at the moment."

"A good deed to cover up the real intentions," Lil Smoke said.

"And intention is only counted if one acts upon it and I didn't," Yasir claimed.

"I don't respect this, Yasir. I'm sorry."

"Do what you feel but know for every action, there is a reaction."

"This is why I'm here now," Lil Smoke said before lifting his pistol.

Boc, Boc, Boc, Boc, Boc, Boc, Boc …

Yasir's body shook as blood poured out the little holes in his chest from the 10mm auto jacketed hollow point bullets that travels through a person's body.

Seeing Yasir eyes closed, Lil Smoke got a little emotional, but he had no more tears to shed. Especially, over a nigga that crossed his brother and faked as if he was a loyal nigga.

Lil Smoke left thinking what he would tell Nafee because this was going to crush him. He figured the best bet would be to put it all on Khadija since she was going crazy anyway.

***

Khadija saw Lil Smoke leave Yasir house and thought if it was perfect time to kill him, but she really wanted to save him for last.

Seeing the Bentley pull off and after hearing all the gunfire, she was thirsty to find out what just happened. Khadija snuck into the house.

It didn't take long for her to find Yasir's body filled with bullet holes with his neck slumped on his pillow.

"Damn, he is Savage's brother." Khadija laughed, leaving happy Lil Smoke finished her job. At first, she planned to let Yasir live and focus on Lil Smoke but men like Yasir never gave up until they felt as if they achieved victory. She came back to finish the job.

She wondered how this would play out if Lil Smoke and Yasir's son Nafee were best friends. Khadija planned to throw salt in the game.

***

University of Miami, Miami

Alina cuddled in her living room, watching a movie, and eating ice cream. She was trying to clear her thoughts, which been cloudy since hearing Royal's phone conversation.

Doing a few days of thinking, Alina came up with a decision to stick with morals. It was either family or a man she loved but just met. In her culture, family was everything.

The knock at her door took her attention away from the good movie. She put on her cotton robe to get the door. Jasmine was at her new boyfriend's room across campus getting some dick, so she wasn't expecting her back this soon.

Opening the door, her heart raced. She was seeing the person that she wasn't ready to see.

"I did something to you?" Lil Smoke asked.

"No, but it's a bad time," Alina said as if she was having company over.

"It's like that?"

"Please, I just need time to think," she stated seriously.

"We can do it together because I love you," he said. She started to cry, and he figured out there had to be something more.

"Can I ask you something and I need you to be honest."

"What up? Anything, baby."

"Would you turn on your loved ones for me?" She looked in his eyes for any flaws or lies.

"Yes, I would. Without a doubt in my mind because I really love you from the deepest part of my heart," Lil Smoke told her, holding Alina's tiny little hands.

"You're in danger."

"I know. My life always in danger."

"No, you don't understand. This is a different type of danger," she said

"What do you mean, Alina? I don't get it."

"The Cartel is trying to kill you and Lil Trap," she said.

"Alina, are you sure? Who is telling you all this shit?"

"A man named Royal is trying to kill you for someone you killed named KVon." She saw Lil Smoke look at her sideways as if Alina was playing the field about to snake him.

"How do you know all this" Are you the fucking police or something?" He hoped Alina wasn't the pigs.

"Royal is my brother that I told you about, leaving out the part that he's a Cartel boss," she told him.

"This can't be fucking real." Lil Smoke felt like he got slapped with a bag of bricks.

"I'm sorry, baby. I didn't want you to judge me if I told you my family is a fucking Cartel family."

"Alina, that's not the point. It's about being honest and upfront because now look."

"I didn't know you was a kingpin dealer and a fucking serial killer," she spat back.

"So, what now? You going to kill me," he said, seeing her dig in her purse.

"I just bought an engagement ring because I wanted to ask you to marry me to let you know I picked a side."

"You don't have to do that, Alina."

"Yes, I do. You don't understand the Cartel. It's one-sided and I choose you. I'm going to sleep. Walk yourself out." Alina walked to her room, feeling a little upset as Lil Smoke left at a loss of words.

Chapter 46
Overtown, Miami

When Lil Smoke walked into the crib, he heard cries coming from the kitchen area and he had a feeling who it was.

"Nafee, what's happened, bruh? You straight?"

"They killed him," Nafee said, wiping his nose.

"Who what the fuck you talking about, bro?" Lil Smoke played his role like an outstanding actor.

"She killed daddy. I just came from the morgue to identify his body."

"Fuck!" Lil Smoke yelled, punching the wall almost breaking his fist.

"It had to be that assassin bitch, bro. I can feel that shit, bro. Daddy ain't deserve to die like that," Nafee said, trying to hold himself together.

"Lil Smoke thought if he only knew how much Yasir deserved the death he got.

"We finna figure all this shit out, bro. Trust me. Just get some sleep so you can be focused. She going to pop up again. Trust that, bruh." Lil Smoke saw Nafee nod.

"I love you, bro. It's just me and you left," Nafee told him as Lil Smoke felt a strike of guilt.

"We family, cuz. I got us."

"I know. I'm just thankful to have you in my life."

"Allah knows best." Lil Smoke walked to his room, thinking about Alina and Nafee. It was all too much for him to take in all at once.

Thinking about a next move, it had to be a checkmate because he realized the odds were really stacked against him.

***

Liberty City, Miami

Solana did a whole day of soul searching and came up with a lots of info on her sister and why she been moving the way she has for years.

Today, Solana followed Jynx around all day and saw her sister sell drugs to thugs all over Miami and outskirt cities.

Solana wasn't even shocked because for years, she always had a feeling Jynx was doing something. Jynx told Solana she was still spending her late husband JoJo's money he left.

Since her parents' death, Solana knew there had to be more of a reason for their brutal slaughter.

Lil Trap was on his way to meet her at a nearby park so she could talk with him and get his advice about some things.

Finding out Jynx sold drugs didn't surprise her, but when they got shot at by a bunch of Mexicans, Solana sought help to figure out how deep Jynx really was. And if her life is safe.

Knowing Lil Trap sold drugs and was doing it big; she knew his input on the situation would but on point.

Lil Trap's car creeped into the lot, and she was happy to see him. It's been a couple of days since they been together.

"You look cute." Lil Trap walked up to her in the sundress, giving her a hug and squeezing that soft fat ass he loved.

"You so nasty."

"Always, what you been up to?"

"Trying to stay levelheaded and put some things together," she replied.

"To be real, me too."

"I wanted to ask you something from the outside looking in." She took a seat next to the park's monkey bars, where a couple of kids played.

"Okay, I'm listening."

"A family member you know, and love has been living a double life for years. They may be the reason your parents live a dangerous life and yours could be at risk. How would you feel?" She looked deep in his eyes for an answer.

"I would demand the truth and get a full understanding of what's really going on. Then, decide to either cut them off to protect myself. Or I would ride for them."

"Even if there a selfish bitch."

"You can only be the judge of that, Solana," he told her.

"Facts."

"Don't stress yourself with the next person affairs. Life is short and people out here dying every day," Lil Trap said

"I saw Nafee post a pic of his dad. Did he really get killed?"

"Yeah, he's sick right now, babe. To keep it a band, shit getting crazy with us. I'ma need you to be safe," he said.

"I got God on my side."

"You need this on your side." Lil Trap handed her a 380 special handgun.

Solana put it inside her designer purse as she looked around. "I don't even know how to use a gun, Travis?"

"I'ma teach you. Just aim and pull the trigger. Easy"

"That's all?" She sounded surprised. "I will, but I got to go to college. I'ma stop by your crib after to get some dick," she said, smiling and rubbing his thigh.

"I'll be waiting for you."

"Ass naked?"

"Yeah, I know you a super freak. I'll be naked, baby." Lil Trap kissed her lips as they talked for a few more minutes.

***

Dade County, Miami

Royal stared at all the photos on the kitchen table that he just received from his private investigator, who he also hired as Alina's personal guard that she didn't know about.

He just wanted to protect his little sister but looking at the pics, he wished he never did it because his heart wouldn't feel betrayed right now.

The photos was Alina with Lil Smoke hugged up in places all over the city. Clubs, beaches, restaurants, and her college.

Royal couldn't risk his life or empire over Alina and there was a big chance she could have put Lil Smoke on about how he was KVon's plug.

His guard Big Rulo waited on his boss to say something for twenty-five minutes now.

"Kill her."

"You sure, boss?"

"Yes, go to her school and kill the bitch. Try to make it clean and easy. I don't want her to suffer," Royal told his main guard.

"Yes sir."

"Thank you." Royal leaned back, smoking a cigar, and thinking how he was about to have his sister's blood on his hands.

***

Atlanta, GA

Jynx came out to Atlanta so she could meet with her main client, Lil D, who had Atlanta under his control.

Lil D walked into the pizza shop in the underground mall, where she was awaiting him for ten minutes now.

"What's going on, beautiful?" Lil D asked, giving Jynx a hug and smelling her sweet perfume.

"How's life? I like your chain," Jynx said, looking at his choker around Lil D's neck.

"Something light, shawty."

"Thanks for coming on time because my flight leaves in one hour."

"Spend some time out here, damn. The only time I saw you enjoy life was the same night I met your sexy ass in Club Onyx," Lil D said, taking a slice of her pizza.

"Shit is crazy right now. We at war with another Cartel family and some little niggas out in Miami but Lil Smoke and his boys are giving us a run for the money," she said, seeing Lil D's body movement change a little in his seat.

"Miami is one hell of a city, but you got to be on point and focus on your bag," Lil D said, thinking about Lil Smoke because the two of them had been bonding hard.

"It's hard out there right now. Someone just tried to kill me and my sister last week."

"Damn Jynx, a few months ago you never had this problem until this new plug." Lil D confirmed.

"Your right, Lil D, but his prices and equity is making us both rich."

"Facts but sometimes it's not even about the money," Lil D explained to her.

"You got a strong point, but everything should be in play for you," Jynx said, referring to his drugs.

"I'ma have my people check on it when I leave here. The money is at the same spot as always. I hope to see you soon." Lil D stood up to leave.

"Damn, no hugs?" She asked.

"Next time, shawty. One is enough"

"Okay." She laughed but feeling something off about his vibe today.

***

Downtown, Miami
Days later

Emma was in the clinic to see why she missed her period and been feeling very sick for three days now. Emma checked her purse for her iPhone and realized it was in the car. She got up, rushing out to the garage across the street.

Life was exalt for Emma beside the fact that tomorrow, Nafee had to bury his dad and remain strong. She did her best to comfort him and show how much Emma really cared for her boo. Being around Nafee and his friends gave Emma a different outlook on life.

When she got to her car in the garage parking lot, Emma took the phone off the charger and shut the door, turning around to see a gun pointed in her face by the man she loved to death.

"Father?" Emma couldn't believe her dad was on the other side of the gun.

"You little bitch. You tried to kill me," Umer told her dressed in all black.

Umer been following Emma since this morning when he saw her at a IHOP food spot. Umer left D.C. just to come find Emma because after spending weeks of thinking of who would want to kill him, Emma popped up in his head.

"What are you talking about? I would never try to kill you."

"Stop lying." He slapped her with the 9mm, knocking Emma to the floor crying in pain and losing a tooth.

"Father, I swear. I would never try to kill you or nobody else," she claimed as Umer laughed.

"It was either you or Khadija and one thing I know about her, is she don't miss. I remember when you was a kid. I took you out to shoot and it was sad. You missed every shot," he said.

"I've done nothing, father. I don't know what you're speaking of. Just let me go," Emma pleaded for her life, knowing Umer was heartless.

"That's not going to happen today, baby girl. I don't want to regret not killing you years from now when I find out it was my little princess trying kill me the whole time."

"But I –"

Boc, Boc, Boc, Boc …

Umer blew her brains out on her front tires and walked off to a truck where his goons awaited him. Umer could have sent his men to kill Emma, but he made himself a promise to kill blood on his own behalf.

Chapter 47
South Miami

Yasir funeral was held in an Islamic mosque. A Janazah for Yasir was performed, which is the proper way a Muslim male and female should be buried.

Nafee and Lil Smoke got done praying behind a local middle eastern imama, who gave the delighted ceremony.

Lil Smoke knew Nafee had a lot on his plate now, with Emma's death hitting the news last night.

They found Emma's dead body slumped next to her car tire with a body bag over her. Lil Smoke had no type of idea who was closing in on them, but he felt the heat.

During the ceremony, Lil Smoke saw a dark skin, beautiful woman in the back. Her sex appeal spoke foreign. She looked African and then his mind flashed to the Khadija chick, which made him look back in a discreet way, but she was gone.

"I'm ready to go," Nafee said, trying to stay strong but losing two people he loved back to back was hard on anyone.

"Okay, I'ma stick around for a minute. Something caught my attention," Lil Smoke says with a conscious look, thinking about the beautiful woman and if she was still around.

"I'll be at home."

"Bet," Lil Smoke replied.

Nafee walked to his car after greeting a group of Muslims standing outside. When he got to the car, there was on note sitting between the windshield wipers.

The front read your eyes only and he got in the car as curiosity entered his thoughts as he read it.

I'm the person you've been looking for. My name is Khadija, and this letter should answer all your questions. I didn't kill you father, but I did whip his as. The day I planned to kill him, someone had already did. That somebody I saw leaving your dad's house was Lil Smoke. I swear to Allah. He killed him for trying to set up Savage, something you don't know about. Next issue, you was dating my sister, Emma and our father killed her, but no worries, I'ma handle him myself. Trust me. I will see you soon and have no doubt that I'm trying to kill you and Lil Smoke, but I thought you should know the truth. Emma really liked you.

Nafee had a fierce inhumane look on his face as he saw Lil Smoke walking out the Mosque with a smile.

"Bitch ass nigga." Nafee grabbed his weapon from under his seat and got out the car with one thing on his brain.

Boc … Boc … Boc … Boc …

Lil Smoke ducked when seeing a bullet strike the Imam in the heart that he was just talking to. He saw Nafee coming at him, so he pulled his gun out and got busy back.

Boom, Boom, Boom, Boom, Boom, Boom …

"What's up with you, nigga!" Lil Smoke yelled as Nafee weaved his bullets.

Nafee wasn't talking, just trying to talk Lil Smoke out as he dipped back into the Mosque at the sounds of cop cars. Nafee got in his car as people scattered all over the place, scared to death and praying the Imam made it through. Lil Smoke snuck out the back, making his way into people's backyards. He was confused but had to get away. He decided to go to Alina's school, calling an Uber.

***

Miami University, Miami

Alina just read the text from Lil Smoke, who said he was on his way to her crib. She got out of bed to get dressed, thinking if something was wrong with him.

There was a bang at the door, and she thought how fast Lil Smoke got to her, but Alina figured he was close when he sent the text.

"What's wrong –" Alina answered the door, seeing Big Rulo push her into her crib, slamming the front door.

Alina swung on the big man, but he easily placed her in a headlock to calm her crazy ass down because she started wilding.

"Relax, Alina. I'm not here to hurt you," Big Rulo told her.

Alina calmed down and he let her go as she fixed the Louis Vuitton top that she rocked.

"What the fuck do you want then, Rulo?"

"Royal sent me to kill you and I won't do it, but Alina, he's going to have you killed and me. It's because of your boyfriend or whoever he is to you. Royal feels betrayed," Big Rulo told her.

"I know it," Alina said, scared now because out of all people, she knew how Royal was.

"You have to go far, Alina." Big Rulo heard a noise behind him. Boom, Boom, Boom …

"Oh my God …" Alina screamed seeing Rulo's head explode.

"Pack your shit. We have to go hurry up," Lil Smoke said, stepping over the dead man. Lil Smoke heard voices outside the door and didn't want to take no risks just in case Alina's life was at risk.

"Everything is packed," she said, rushing to get her Gucci luggage, already prepared for this.

Alina and Lil Smoke rushed to his Bentley, looking around just in case Royal sent some more goons to take them out.

Once in the car, Lil Smoke spun out of the parking lot with a Draco in his lap that he got from under his seat.

"What the fuck is going on, babe? This dude just told me Royal sent him to kill me," Alina said.

"Your brother must know."

"Yes, but he got the right bitch. I ain't finna let him carry my casket like he did my aunties and uncles because they didn't want to work for him. He killed four of them in Mexico," she told Lil Smoke, who got on the expressway and headed to his hideout that bought last month just in case of an emergency.

"This going to get crazy, baby and I'ma need you to listen and pay attention now more than ever," he told her.

"Of course, papi. We a team and the only way to get through this is plot, plan, and attack together."

"I don't know about attacks, but we can plan and plot all day, babe." Lil Smoke got off downtown where the secret condo was located.

"I killed before." She saw him laugh.

"Okay and I'm a ghostbuster," he replied.

"I was raised in the Cartel. That's all I saw my whole life fa'real."

"Shit, you should've seen the look on your face when I shot the Big Rulo fucker in the head," he told her.

"That was different. I ain't expect you to pop up on us like that."

"I know." Lil Smoke pulled in a private parking lot after spinning the block twice to make sure nobody was on their ass.

"When did you move out here?" Alina asked, getting out of the car.

"This was for only hiding out cases and this is one because me and Nafee just got into a big shoot out at the funeral," Lil Smoke said, walking in through the back entrance.

"Ain't no way. I can't believe this, Lil Smoke. This is too much."

"I know, but the nigga just started shooting at me for no reason. I think he found out that I killed his dad." Lil Smoke saw the look on Alina's face.

"That was like your father too, right?"

"Yeah."

"I don't understand that babe. Maybe I'm missing something here." Alina was starting to think if her life in Lil Smoke's hands could be trusted because he been killing everybody, he seemed close to.

"It's a long story."

"Oh, we have a long time to talk about it," she said, following him into the empty crib. Alina saw nothing except a carpet and drapes. No furniture or no TV's.

"We going to need to fix this spot up, but right now, I got to run and get the drugs from the stash."

"I'll be here, I guess."

"At least we got a bed."

"I hope you ain't have no bitches in there," she joked but serious.

"I'll see you later and I'll never cheat on you babe." He left the condo.

Chapter 48
Georgetown, D.C.

Umer had a new mini mansion in the upper class section of D.C. surrounded by security guards he brought out from Africa. This coming weekend, Umer planned to go back home because he felt like his job was done.

Killing Emma wasn't the best feeling, but he knew she was the one trying to kill him. There couldn't be nobody else who would try their hand without knowing the outcome.

He came into the kitchen, looking for a late night snack while his team of trained shooters watched TV inside the living room. Some were sleep upstairs.

Umer donned an expensive Versace rope. He dug inside his freezer looking for something to warm.

Tat …Tat …Tat …Tat … Tat …

Umer dropped to the floor at the sounds of the gunfire. He was now crawling on the floor to peep his head around the corner of his counter.

He watched someone dressed in all black, shooting every guard in the living room in their head before another squad of Africa goons ran in the room shooting.

Seeing the gunmen jump over the couch and popping up like jack in the box firing, he knew what time it was for him. Umer crawled into the bottom cabinet to hide as the gunfire back and forth sounded like drum rolls.

Tat, Tat, Tat, Tat, Tat, Tat, Tat, Tat, Tat…

Listening to silence for twenty seconds, he pushed the cabinet door open a little to hear any type of movement. When he heard nothing, Umer thought it was over. He crawled out in a slow pace like a tiger hunting prey and closing in on it.

"Take another crawl and I'll blow your fucking ass off," the voice said, coming from behind Umer.

"Khadija?"

"You know who it was bitch," she said, walking in front of him.

"Baby girl, what's going on?" Umer said, looking up at her with pity eyes.

"You killed my little sister, Umer. That's the second one and I won't be your third," Khadija told him, hearing his grown man cries.

"She tried to kill me," Umer claimed.

"What? She would never do such a thing. She doesn't even know the first thing about killing and you should know that."

"It had to be her, Khadija, if it wasn't you. She tracked my moves and could have took me out." Umer was starting to think he had fucked up and was missing something.

"Okay, think what you want was Khadija last words.

Tat, Tat, Tat, Tat, Tat, Tat, Tat, Tat...

She felt so good pulling the trigger. Khadija shot him ten more times.

All of Umer's guards were laid out dead, except one trying to crawl to the door but Khadija put two in his back before walking out the nice house she liked.

On her trip back to Miami, all she could think about was her next mission, which had been long overdue.

***

Pork N Beans Projects, Miami

Nafee called Rakeem and told him to meet him in the back of Rakeem PJs so they could talk real quick. Since having the shootout with Lil Smoke, he been on one. Nafee was parked outside their crib all night, waiting for Lil Smoke to kill him but he never came.

There wasn't a doubt in his mind that made him second guess Lil Smoke killing Yasir. The main reason was how funny Lil Smoke had been moving since Yasir's death. Nafee peeped how his so-called brother never shed one tear or a drop of emotion, which bugged him, but he now knew why.

Rakeem rushed out the back of one tall building that he had been selling drugs out of and made 17,000 in two hours off grams.

"You good, bruh?"

"Nah, this nigga backdoored me," Nafee said, pissed off.

"Who?" Rakeem knew his brother lost his dad and girl, so he was going through it right now.

"Lil Smoke."

"The nigga who our brother?"

"Yeah, you met him last week, but I found out he shot my dad. So, it's on now," Nafee said.

"Damn, why would he do that, bruh?"

"I don't know why or give a fuck. He lucky I missed him when I tried to knock his block off," Says Nafee.

"Y'all shot it out, cuz?"

"Hell yeah, right in front of the mosque." Nafee pulled out a Newport to smoke and he didn't even smoke.

"I'm with you, bro. Trust me. We a team, bruh. I started with you so that's how I'ma finish," Rakeem said, letting Nafee know he had his loyalty.

"That's all I need to know bro; Lil Smoke took a little drugs but I'ma find a new plug. I got a plan, bruh. Give me a few weeks," Nafee said, getting in his car. He couldn't believe how life will change.

"Aight, dog. I'm here for you." Rakeem walked back into the building.

***

Liberty City, Miami

Lil Smoke, Lil Trap, and Bowy all sat in the new Tahoe truck Lil Smoke just brought to stay low key in because too many people knew about the Bentley truck.

"Nafee on some weird shit. He's been parked in front of the crib for a whole day," Lil Trap said trying to figure out what's really going on because both men were moving funny.

"It's a lot of old shit going on. I called Rakeem ten minutes ago. He told me to never call him again. I was just checking on him," Bowy stated from the backseat of the parked truck.

"I killed his father," Lil Smoke said.

"Yo' what?" Lil Trap thought he heard wrong

"Yasir tried to get my brother before his death, bruh. I had to do something," Lil Smoke told them.

"I feel you," Bowy said.

"So, what it is now?" Lil Trap said.

"He tried to kill me," Lil Smoke said

"Nafee bitch ass?" Lil Trap shot back shocked.

"Yeah bro, it's lit now and if I know Nafee like I think, he going to form a team and go against us." Lil Smoke knew how Nafee thought. He was real smart and sneaky.

"Rakeem," Bowy said.

"Let him do whatever. We ready," Lil Trap stated ready to ride.

"Aight but don't underestimate him, please," Lil Smoke told his crew before they exited his car with a new gameplan in mind.

***

Downtown, Miami

Jynx wanted Lil D's people to drop her off the money in a truck company parking lot next to a post office. It was 8pm and his people should've been there 15 minutes ago. She called Lil D to only get a voicemail.

Finally, a car was driving into the lot. She saw two men in the Impala, when the car lights shut off, staring at her. Lil D always had his goons drop her off the money after he got the drugs. She trusted him that much.

The two men got out of the car, and she saw a shiny glimpse of something and acted.

Boc, Boc, Boc, Boc, Boc, Boc …

Boom, Boom, Boom, Boom, Boom …

The men both fired back at Jynx. One of them hit her good in her side, making her body fly into the floor.

Jynx dropped her weapon by a mistake, due to her pain, as the two men ran down on her to finish the hit Lil D sent.

"This for Lil D, bitch!" One of the gunners said as they both stood over her.

Jynx had never been so close to death in her life, and she was at peace with it, looking into the shiny weapons.

"Suck my clit bitch."

"You're a bad bitch but I love money more," one of them said.

Bloc ...Bloc ... Bloc ... Bloc ... Bloc ... Bloc ...

Jynx saw the shooter's body drop, as a man she could barely see, lifted her up off the ground in his arms. He carried her to his car.

"Hold tight, you going to make it," Nafee told her, rushing her to a hospital and speeding through the Miami streets.

"Who are you?" Jynx asked, laying in the back, holding her gunshot wound in pain.

"That doesn't matter right now. I want you to focus on putting pressure on that wound beautiful," Nafee told her.

Nafee was driving by thinking of a plan to kill Lil Smoke when he saw two men about to kill a woman and that was something he wouldn't have been able to live with, especially a civilian. He never saw a woman beautiful as Jynx, but she looked familiar somewhat. Her sex appeal was something rare.

"Thank you," Jynx whispered feeling dizzy as he pulled into the hospital and rushed her in, saying a stray bullet hit her on a highway. The doctors rushed to help, and Nafee stayed, feeling bad and hoping she'd make it.

Romell Tukes

Chapter 49
Memorial Jackson Hospital, Miami

Nafee had been at the hospital all day since coming back after dropping Jynx off. He became too tired and slept in his car last night. There was something special about Jynx he liked, and the way Nafee felt with her in his arms seemed so right.

The woman did look familiar but that didn't matter right now. He would question who she was later, not today.

Lil Smoke had been on his mind heavy lately Every time he closed his eyes, Lil Smoke was all he thought about.

With Rakeem on his team, he knew shit was about to get nasty when he cleared head and put some plots together. There was no doubt Lil Smoke had Bowy and Lil Trap on his team, but Nafee knew how to play that and build an army once he found a plug.

"Nurse, the lady that was shot last night in her side. Is she okay?" Nafee asked a young man in scrubs, getting sick of waiting.

"The pretty lady who pulled through?" The nurse knew exactly who he was speaking of because Jynx alluring features caught his attention.

"Yes."

"She is in the ICU room 162 doing well. You can go see her. Visiting hours are in right now so you good," The nurse told him before walking to the elevator to handle some business.

"Thanks." Nafee walked through the double doors, a little nervous for whatever reason. He had butterflies in his stomach.

Once close to the room, he saw his phone was ringing. It was Rakeem but Nafee knew what he wanted. Rakeem told him last night he would put a team together in less than 24 hours and Nafee knew his brother could make it happen.

Nafee texted him in thirty minutes. He planned to call but right now he was a little busy. He knocked on the door.

Jynx looked to him to see who the fuck was at her door because she wasn't in a good mood after being shot twice. Nafee walked in and she had no clue who the man was standing before her.

"Hey, how can I help you?" Jynx asked.

"I just wanted to make sure you were okay after last night."

"Oh, you're the dude that saved me. It was real dark out, but I owe you my life," she told him, making him smile.

"I was headed somewhere while I really wasn't on nothing. I was just driving around to clear my head and that's when I saw your situation," he said.

"That's so sweet. My name is Jynx."

"I'm Nafee. Nice to meet you. I'm glad you're okay, though."

"Thanks to you but have I saw you somewhere?" She asked, realizing he looked like a person she recently saw somewhere but it was not connecting.

"Maybe, but I asked myself the same thing," Nafee said, seeing Jynx daze off into the ceiling.

Jynx now knew who he was. Nafee and his crew shot up the car show a while back and she just realized that was the Lil Smoke kid Royal recently told her all about the other day.

"You Lil Smoke people." Jynx gave him an angry look.

"Don't ever say that. Fuck him. I'm my own man. He dead to me." Nafee's voice raised.

"Sorry, but you did used to be with him, right? Because if so, I saw you before." Jynx tried to fish for shit because if she could get to Lil Smoke, Mucho and Lura would be an easy kill.

"Yes, we was family until he killed my dad but now I'ma kill him."

"That's foul. I'm sorry to hear about your loss, Nafee."

"Wait, who the fuck are you?" Nafee asked.

"I'm the person who going to help you complete our mission." She smiled

"Mission? I think we are on two different types of missions, Jynx," said Nafee, looking at her grin like the devil.

"Oh no Nafee, we have the same plans and I think I will be able to be a big help."

"To me?"

"Yes, I'll explain more when we get out of here, which is now." Jynx took all the IVs out of her arms and unplugged the machines as they beeped nonstop.

"You should wait until the nurses clear you, Jynx. You're still bleeding" Nafee saw blood stains on her gown.

"I'ma grown ass bitch. Pass me my clothes," she said, looking at her bloody outfit she came into the hospital in.

"That shit bloody. You need to lay down," he said, seeing her get up and walking toward the door next to him.

"Get the fuck out the way or come with me so I can explain everything to you," she told him, walking pass Nafee.

Two nurses tried to stop Jynx, but she cursed them out and left anyway. Nafee had no choice but to follow her hard head ass outside.

"Your stubborn," Nafee told her, taking her to his car.

"Take me to Collins Ave and you're not my father," she told him, climbing in the passenger seat.

"You going to shopping in a hospital gown?"

"Yep, now drive before the police come to ask dumb ass questions," she said.

"Yes boss," he joked as she gave him the evil eye.

After shopping, Jynx explained to him who she was and what her position was as a boss under Royal.

Nafee couldn't believe he was talking to the opp of Lil Smoke's plug. This made him connect with her more and take her offer. By the end of that day, Jynx and Nafee were business partners. It was her way of paying him back for saving her life.

***

Golden Beach, Miami

Dr. Akbar heard the front doorbell ring and left his library, rushing downstairs for the pod man to come clean the pods in the back.

Opening the door, Dr. Akbar's warm smile vanished real quick, seeing the gun pointed at his heart by his worst nightmare.

"Hey Doc," Khadija said, dressed in a Islamic gourmet and a hijab wrapped around her face.

"First my wife, now me?" Dr. Akbar knew it was over for him.

"Yes, and next will be your beautiful daughter." She confirmed.

"Please don't harm my daughter. She has nothing to do with this and she don't know anything," Dr. Akbar pleaded.

"So, are you going to tell me?" Khadija asked and the doc knew what she was talking about.

"I have no clue as to what you're referring to Khadija, but just know you won't get away with this."

"You're in the wrong space to send threats, big guy."

"May Allah leave your soul in the burning fire," he told her.

"Thank you for the kind blessings, Doc." Khadija told him before pulling the trigger with ease.

Boc, Boc, Boc, Boc, Boc, Boc, Boc, Boc, …

"Perfect fall." Khadija says when Dr. Akbar's body hit the floor, walking off enjoying the sunny day. She was thinking about going to the beach to sit next to some water.

***

South, Miami

Mucho checked his Richard Muller watch, hoping he would make it to the airport on time as the traffic on the bridge was backed up today.

The two guards were starting to get frustrated. Mucho rolled the bulletproof windows down to get some air and smoke a cigar to calm his nerves.

"This sucks," Mucho said.

"I hate rush hour," the driver said.

"Next time, don't take this fucking bridge. Better yet, who the fuck told you to take the bridge?" Mucho asked the new driver he just hired last week. He had to kill his last one.

"I thought it would be faster, boss," the bald-headed Mexican man stated.

"Oh, good because today you fired big guy," Mucho said, not trying to hear nothing.

Two black motorcycles pulled up the Mucho's truck window.

Tat, Tat, Tat, Tat, Tat, Tat, Tat, Tat, Tat, Tat, Tat …

Bullets ripped through Mucho's skull, catching him by surprise. The shooters then killed the driver, who set it all up. The passenger crawled out the passenger side of the SUV, trying to spare his own life.

Royal's shooter raced off in traffic to collect the bounty on Mucho's head. Killing a Cartel boss could be an easy million any day. Mucho's new driver was working with the shooters to get a percent of the cut, but things didn't work out in his favor.

***

Miami Beach, Miami
Four days later

Lura waited for Lil Smoke's arrival, which should be shortly. The past couple of days been pressure and grief for Lura after losing Mucho on the bridge.

When she got the news, her life felt like it flipped upside down in a matter of seconds. Lura cried for two days straight with no breaks. She didn't even answer no phone calls from nobody at all, not even her own family calling from Mexico.

Lura spoke to Preslee this morning and she was already on a flight from Mexico. She figured Lil Smoke already knew about Mucho's death because it was the talk of Miami and the world news about a Cartel boss killed by rival Cartels.

Now with Mucho out the picture, she planned to take over what he left, which would be easy. Lura already was basically running the business besides in other states like in Cali and Texas.

Guards were all on heavy guard since Mucho's death and it was going to be like this now that she was calling shots.

Three guards brought Lil Smoke to the backyard gazebo where Lura sat in a rocking chair drinking iced tea.

Lil Smoke walked right up to her and gave her a big hug and squeezed Lura's body, showing genuine affection.

"I heard what happened and I'm so sorry. I called out for two days straight, but I figured you needed that time to get yourself together," he said, sitting next to her. He was so close; it was almost skin to skin.

"Shit happens. Now, I just got to move forward and focus on the family business," she stated strongly.

"That's real but I got something to tell you that I recently found out, but I need you to trust me," he told her, seeing the expression on Lura's face.

"What is it? I hope no more bad news because I'm tired."

"No, it's my girlfriend, Alina. She overheard her brother talking about killing me and told me who he was."

"Okay, you need help?" Lura didn't understand where Lil Smoke was going with this.

"Her brother sent men to kill her once he found out me and Alina was together. I don't even know how he found out," Lil Smoke said, seeing he was about to lose her attention.

"Kill him, then."

"Guess who he is?"

"Jesus … shit, I don't know, Lil Smoke," she replied.

"Royal." Lil Smoke saw Lura's eyes turn red like a real demon.

"Where the fuck is she?" Lura was ready to kill. A brother for a sister.

"Lura, please, she is with us. I swear she wants to kill him also and I know Alina can lead us right to Royal." Lil Smoke saw her shake her head.

"I don't trust it. She could be setting all this up, Lil Smoke. Have you thought about that?"

"Yes, and that is why I put her through my tests, and she passed them all, Lura. I need you to trust me."

"I'ma take your word but don't let your dick cloud your judgment because everything could go downhill." She warned him.

"I understand and Nafee is exed out. I'm at war with him because I found out his father was sent to kill Savage and that made me feel betrayed. There was no way I could have let that shit slide," Lil Smoke told her.

"You did right but things are heating up. I'ma keep a few guards with you at all times. I need you to be protected. I can't lose you either," she said emotionally, and he didn't have a reply. It became an awkward moment.

"I'ma go. I just came to check on you but next week, I'll be ready for the load to land. My boy, Lil D from Atlanta on deck with us. He just killed the chick you got into a shootout with," he told Lura, who look surprised.

"When did he kill Jynx?"

"Last week. This whole time, I never knew his plug was Jynx. When he told me she was talking about me, he called, and we planned to rob Jynx. We hit her up when it was time to pick the money up for the product," he explained.

"You sure she's dead?"

"I believe so."

"I'ma make sure," Lura stated.

"Aight, call me if you need me, beautiful," Lil Smoke said, seeing her smile as she left.

***

Lil Smoke climbed in the rental car glad Lura accepted Alina before she go crazy over Mucho death and kill everything Royal ever loved, including old teddy bears.

Driving out the outside gates, he answered Lil Trap's call on the car speaker.

"What it do, folk" Lil Trap said, sounding like he was driving in the background.

"On my way to Lil Havana, bruh. What's up with you cuz?"

"Going to a cookout about to pick up Solana," Lil Trap said.

"Damn, you ain't invited me thug?" Lil Smoke pulled up behind an old school Chevy at a red light about to hit the ghetto part of Dade County.

"My bad, bruh. Me and Bowy was just talking about asking you, but we know you ain't coming to no cookout. You feel me, bruh?" Lil Trap says and Lil Smoke agreed as two trucks pulled up to his door side.

Lil Smoke looked over his shoulder and ducked as AK-47 assault rifles.

Tat, Tat, Tat, Tat, Tat, Tat, Tat, Tat, Tat, Tat … Tat, Tat, Tat, Tat, Tat, Tat, Tat, Tat, Tat, Tat…

Nafee and Rakeem pulled off after hitting Lil Smoke's car up with thirty rounds, knowing he was dead. They had their eye on him all day and Nafee knew it was now or never.

A black car with black tints raced up to Lil Smoke's car and jumped out, taking him out and tossing him in back of the car driving off, hoping to save the young man's life.

***

Golden Beach, Miami
One day later

Lil Smoke felt like he was having Deja-Vu over him crying.

"Oh, my God, you made it," Scarlit cried after performing surgery on him all night and day. She took out all seven bullets, except one she left in his back.

"They got me good?" Lil Smoke's whole body felt numb from the pain meds.

"That doesn't matter right now. You're alive." She was so happy.

"Where is your dad?" He asked, seeing her get more emotional.

"The other day I came home for the week and to tell daddy I graduated, and his body was lying in a puddle of blood, dead," Scarlit said, taking off her mask and gloves.

"Damn, I'm sorry, Scarlit."

"It's okay. I just want you to heal because this time you are in bad condition. It will take time to walk because you took five shots to your hip bone and joints," she told him.

"Damn, wait!" He yelled as she turned to leave.

"Who brought me here? Somebody saved me. I remember him. He was in all black," Lil Smoke said.

"I told you. I don't know. When I heard someone bang on the door, I was cleaning my dad's house. I saw you laying there on the wall. I rushed you down here on a stretcher and went to work on you," she told him before leaving.

Lil Smoke's mind was spinning before the meds put him right out.

***

Broward County, Miami

Khadija got off her new motorcycle she just copped today for the trip she had set for tomorrow. Khadija was going to Kentucky to live and get the fuck out of Miami for good. She lost everything for nothing. Walking into her hotel room, she turned on the light switch, but it wasn't working. Khadija heard a gun cock. She now knew why.

"It's been a while, Khadija. You shot me ten times but luckily, I had on a vest. Dr. Akbar saved me. He was on standby at the gravesite the day you tried to kill me. It was all a part of my plan," the voice said as Khadija's heart fell to the floor, listening to Savage's voice.

"Savage, I won't beg for my life, but I do respect you. If anybody is going to kill me, then I'm glad it's a man I thought was dead," she joked before Savage shot her ten times in her head. Savage walked out of the hotel to go check on Lil Smoke. He saved his life yesterday after seeing the same SUV that was tailing him, air his car out. Savage had been playing the cut, but he was back and ready to proclaim his throne with the help of his little brother whenever he pulled through…

To Be Continued…
Life of a Savage 5
Coming Soon

Romell Tukes

Lock Down Publications and Ca$h Presents assisted publishing packages.

BASIC PACKAGE $499
Editing
Cover Design
Formatting

UPGRADED PACKAGE $800
Typing
Editing
Cover Design
Formatting

ADVANCE PACKAGE $1,200
Typing
Editing
Cover Design
Formatting
Copyright registration
Proofreading
Upload book to Amazon

LDP SUPREME PACKAGE $1,500
Typing
Editing
Cover Design
Formatting
Copyright registration
Proofreading
Set up Amazon account
Upload book to Amazon
Advertise on LDP Amazon and Facebook page

***Other services available upon request. Additional charges may apply

Lock Down Publications
P.O. Box 944
Stockbridge, GA 30281-9998
Phone # 470 303-9761

Submission Guideline

Submit the first three chapters of your completed manuscript to ldpsubmissions@gmail.com, subject line: Your book's title. The manuscript must be in a .doc file and sent as an attachment. Document should be in Times New Roman, double spaced and in size 12 font. Also, provide your synopsis and full contact information. If sending multiple submissions, they must each be in a separate email.

Have a story but no way to send it electronically? You can still submit to LDP/Ca$h Presents. Send in the first three chapters, written or typed, of your completed manuscript to:

LDP: Submissions Dept
Po Box 944
Stockbridge, Ga 30281

DO NOT send original manuscript. Must be a duplicate.

Provide your synopsis and a cover letter containing your full contact information.

Thanks for considering LDP and Ca$h Presents.

NEW RELEASES

JACK BOYS VS DOPE BOYS 2 by ROMELL TUKES

MURDA WAS THE CASE by ELIJAH R. FREEMAN

KING OF THE TRENCHES 3 by GHOST & TRANAY AD-

AMS

JACK BOYS VS DOPE BOYS 3 by ROMELL TUKES

LIFE OF A SAVAGE 4 by ROMELL TUKES

Romell Tukes

Coming Soon from Lock Down Publications/Ca$h Presents

BLOOD OF A BOSS **VI**

SHADOWS OF THE GAME II

TRAP BASTARD II

By **Askari**

LOYAL TO THE GAME **IV**

By **T.J. & Jelissa**

TRUE SAVAGE **VIII**

MIDNIGHT CARTEL IV

DOPE BOY MAGIC IV

CITY OF KINGZ III

NIGHTMARE ON SILENT AVE II

THE PLUG OF LIL MEXICO II

CLASSIC CITY II

By **Chris Green**

BLAST FOR ME **III**

A SAVAGE DOPEBOY III

CUTTHROAT MAFIA III

DUFFLE BAG CARTEL VII

HEARTLESS GOON VI

By **Ghost**

A HUSTLER'S DECEIT III

KILL ZONE II

BAE BELONGS TO ME III

TIL DEATH II

By **Aryanna**

KING OF THE TRAP III

By **T.J. Edwards**

GORILLAZ IN THE BAY V

3X KRAZY III

Life of a Savage 4

STRAIGHT BEAST MODE III

De'Kari

KINGPIN KILLAZ IV

STREET KINGS III

PAID IN BLOOD III

CARTEL KILLAZ IV

DOPE GODS III

Hood Rich

SINS OF A HUSTLA II

ASAD

RICH $AVAGE III

By Martell Troublesome Bolden

YAYO V

Bred In The Game 2

S. Allen

THE STREETS WILL TALK II

By Yolanda Moore

SON OF A DOPE FIEND III

HEAVEN GOT A GHETTO II

SKI MASK MONEY II

By Renta

LOYALTY AIN'T PROMISED III

By Keith Williams

I'M NOTHING WITHOUT HIS LOVE II

SINS OF A THUG II

TO THE THUG I LOVED BEFORE II

IN A HUSTLER I TRUST II

By Monet Dragun

QUIET MONEY IV

EXTENDED CLIP III

Romell Tukes

THUG LIFE IV

By **Trai'Quan**

THE STREETS MADE ME IV

By **Larry D. Wright**

IF YOU CROSS ME ONCE II

ANGEL IV

By **Anthony Fields**

THE STREETS WILL NEVER CLOSE IV

By **K'ajji**

HARD AND RUTHLESS III

KILLA KOUNTY III

By **Khufu**

MONEY GAME III

By **Smoove Dolla**

JACK BOYS VS DOPE BOYS IV

A GANGSTA'S QUR'AN V

COKE GIRLZ II

COKE BOYS II

LIFE OF A SAVAGE V

By **Romell Tukes**

MURDA WAS THE CASE III

Elijah R. Freeman

THE STREETS NEVER LET GO III

By **Robert Baptiste**

AN UNFORESEEN LOVE IV

By **Meesha**

MONEY MAFIA II

By **Jibril Williams**

QUEEN OF THE ZOO III

Life of a Savage 4

By **Black Migo**

VICIOUS LOYALTY III

By Kingpen

A GANGSTA'S PAIN III

By J-Blunt

CONFESSIONS OF A JACKBOY III

By Nicholas Lock

GRIMEY WAYS III

By Ray Vinci

KING KILLA II

By Vincent "Vitto" Holloway

BETRAYAL OF A THUG II

By Fre$h

THE MURDER QUEENS III

By Michael Gallon

THE BIRTH OF A GANGSTER III

By Delmont Player

TREAL LOVE II

By Le'Monica Jackson

FOR THE LOVE OF BLOOD II

By Jamel Mitchell

RAN OFF ON DA PLUG II

By Paper Boi Rari

HOOD CONSIGLIERE II

By Keese

PRETTY GIRLS DO NASTY THINGS II

By Nicole Goosby

PROTÉGÉ OF A LEGEND II

By Corey Robinson

IT'S JUST ME AND YOU II

Romell Tukes

By Ah'Million
BORN IN THE GRAVE II
By Self Made Tay
FOREVER GANGSTA III
By Adrian Dulan
GORILLAZ IN THE TRENCHES II
By SayNoMore

Available Now

RESTRAINING ORDER **I & II**
By **CA$H & Coffee**
LOVE KNOWS NO BOUNDARIES **I II & III**
By **Coffee**
RAISED AS A GOON I, II, III & IV
BRED BY THE SLUMS I, II, III
BLAST FOR ME I & II
ROTTEN TO THE CORE I II III
A BRONX TALE I, II, III
DUFFLE BAG CARTEL I II III IV V VI
HEARTLESS GOON I II III IV V
A SAVAGE DOPEBOY I II
DRUG LORDS I II III
CUTTHROAT MAFIA I II

Life of a Savage 4

Romell Tukes

AN UNFORESEEN LOVE I II III
By **Meesha**
A GANGSTER'S CODE I &, II III
A GANGSTER'S SYN I II III
THE SAVAGE LIFE I II III
CHAINED TO THE STREETS I II III
BLOOD ON THE MONEY I II III
A GANGSTA'S PAIN I II
By J-Blunt
PUSH IT TO THE LIMIT
By **Bre' Hayes**
BLOOD OF A BOSS **I, II, III, IV, V**
SHADOWS OF THE GAME
TRAP BASTARD
By **Askari**
THE STREETS BLEED MURDER **I, II & III**
THE HEART OF A GANGSTA I II& III
By **Jerry Jackson**
CUM FOR ME I II III IV V VI VII VIII
An **LDP Erotica Collaboration**
BRIDE OF A HUSTLA **I II & II**
THE FETTI GIRLS **I, II& III**
CORRUPTED BY A GANGSTA I, II III, IV
BLINDED BY HIS LOVE
THE PRICE YOU PAY FOR LOVE I, II ,III
DOPE GIRL MAGIC I II III
By **Destiny Skai**
WHEN A GOOD GIRL GOES BAD
By **Adrienne**
THE COST OF LOYALTY I II III

Life of a Savage 4

By Kweli

A GANGSTER'S REVENGE **I II III & IV**

THE BOSS MAN'S DAUGHTERS I II III IV V

A SAVAGE LOVE **I & II**

BAE BELONGS TO ME I II

A HUSTLER'S DECEIT I, II, III

WHAT BAD BITCHES DO I, II, III

SOUL OF A MONSTER I II III

KILL ZONE

A DOPE BOY'S QUEEN I II III

TIL DEATH

By **Aryanna**

A KINGPIN'S AMBITON

A KINGPIN'S AMBITION **II**

I MURDER FOR THE DOUGH

By **Ambitious**

TRUE SAVAGE I II III IV V VI VII

DOPE BOY MAGIC I, II, III

MIDNIGHT CARTEL I II III

CITY OF KINGZ I II

NIGHTMARE ON SILENT AVE

THE PLUG OF LIL MEXICO II

CLASSIC CITY

By **Chris Green**

A DOPEBOY'S PRAYER

By **Eddie "Wolf" Lee**

THE KING CARTEL **I, II & III**

By **Frank Gresham**

THESE NIGGAS AIN'T LOYAL **I, II & III**

By **Nikki Tee**

Romell Tukes

GANGSTA SHYT **I II &III**

By **CATO**

THE ULTIMATE BETRAYAL

By **Phoenix**

BOSS'N UP **I , II & III**

By **Royal Nicole**

I LOVE YOU TO DEATH

By **Destiny J**

I RIDE FOR MY HITTA

I STILL RIDE FOR MY HITTA

By **Misty Holt**

LOVE & CHASIN' PAPER

By **Qay Crockett**

TO DIE IN VAIN

SINS OF A HUSTLA

By **ASAD**

BROOKLYN HUSTLAZ

By **Boogsy Morina**

BROOKLYN ON LOCK I & II

By **Sonovia**

GANGSTA CITY

By **Teddy Duke**

A DRUG KING AND HIS DIAMOND I & II III

A DOPEMAN'S RICHES

HER MAN, MINE'S TOO I, II

CASH MONEY HO'S

THE WIFEY I USED TO BE I II

PRETTY GIRLS DO NASTY THINGS

By Nicole Goosby

TRAPHOUSE KING **I II & III**

Life of a Savage 4

KINGPIN KILLAZ I II III

STREET KINGS I II

PAID IN BLOOD **I II**

CARTEL KILLAZ I II III

DOPE GODS I II

By **Hood Rich**

LIPSTICK KILLAH **I, II, III**

CRIME OF PASSION I II & III

FRIEND OR FOE I II III

By **Mimi**

STEADY MOBBN' **I, II, III**

THE STREETS STAINED MY SOUL I II III

By **Marcellus Allen**

WHO SHOT YA **I, II, III**

SON OF A DOPE FIEND I II

HEAVEN GOT A GHETTO

SKI MASK MONEY

Renta

GORILLAZ IN THE BAY **I II III IV**

TEARS OF A GANGSTA I II

3X KRAZY I II

STRAIGHT BEAST MODE I II

DE'KARI

TRIGGADALE I II III

MURDAROBER WAS THE CASE I II

Elijah R. Freeman

GOD BLESS THE TRAPPERS I, II, III

THESE SCANDALOUS STREETS I, II, III

FEAR MY GANGSTA I, II, III IV, V

THESE STREETS DON'T LOVE NOBODY I, II

Romell Tukes

BURY ME A G I, II, III, IV, V

A GANGSTA'S EMPIRE I, II, III, IV

THE DOPEMAN'S BODYGAURD I II

THE REALEST KILLAZ I II III

THE LAST OF THE OGS I II III

Tranay Adams

THE STREETS ARE CALLING

Duquie Wilson

MARRIED TO A BOSS I II III

By Destiny Skai & Chris Green

KINGZ OF THE GAME I II III IV V VI

Playa Ray

SLAUGHTER GANG I II III

RUTHLESS HEART I II III

By Willie Slaughter

FUK SHYT

By Blakk Diamond

DON'T F#CK WITH MY HEART I II

By Linnea

ADDICTED TO THE DRAMA I II III

IN THE ARM OF HIS BOSS II

By Jamila

YAYO I II III IV

A SHOOTER'S AMBITION I II

BRED IN THE GAME

By S. Allen

TRAP GOD I II III

RICH $AVAGE I II

MONEY IN THE GRAVE I II III

By Martell Troublesome Bolden

Life of a Savage 4

Romell Tukes

Life of a Savage 4

Romell Tukes

by **GHOST & TRANAY ADAMS**

QUEEN OF THE ZOO I II

By **Black Migo**

GRIMEY WAYS I II

By **Ray Vinci**

XMAS WITH AN ATL SHOOTER

By **Ca$h & Destiny Skai**

KING KILLA

By **Vincent "Vitto" Holloway**

BETRAYAL OF A THUG

By **Fre$h**

THE MURDER QUEENS I II

By **Michael Gallon**

TREAL LOVE

By **Le'Monica Jackson**

FOR THE LOVE OF BLOOD

By **Jamel Mitchell**

HOOD CONSIGLIERE

By **Keese**

PROTÉGÉ OF A LEGEND

By **Corey Robinson**

BORN IN THE GRAVE

By **Self Made Tay**

MOAN IN MY MOUTH

By **XTASY**

Life of a Savage 4

BOOKS BY LDP'S CEO, CA$H

TRUST IN NO MAN

TRUST IN NO MAN 2

TRUST IN NO MAN 3

BONDED BY BLOOD

SHORTY GOT A THUG

THUGS CRY

THUGS CRY 2

THUGS CRY 3

TRUST NO BITCH

TRUST NO BITCH 2

TRUST NO BITCH 3

TIL MY CASKET DROPS

RESTRAINING ORDER

RESTRAINING ORDER 2

IN LOVE WITH A CONVICT

LIFE OF A HOOD STAR

XMAS WITH AN ATL SHOOTER

Romell Tukes